Savvy Diva's Take On...

44 DAYS OF RANDOM THOUGHTS & OBSERVATIONS!

By Jahzara,
The Savvy Diva

Savvy Diva's Take On . . . 44 Days of Random Thoughts and Observations!

Copyright © 2011 by Jahzara, the Savvy Diva
Published by **JAHPHUT**
P.O. Box 2540
Washington, DC 20013
www.jahphut.com

ISBN: 0977063038
ISBN-13: 9780977063031
LCCN: 2011921897
*Written by Jahzara, the Savvy Diva, Edited by
Jahphut's Editorial Team and CreateSpace Editors.
Text, Cover, and Graphic Design by CreateSpace.
Printed in the United States of America.*

This book is dedicated
In loving memory
of my father, John,
and my best friend, Tyreese.

And to . . .
My Mommy, my Soul Mate,
my handsome Son and
my beautiful Goddaughter.

I Love You!

Acknowledgements

I wish to thank and acknowledge J. Phillips, D.C. Roberts, Stacy Akerele, and Dr. Meredith Rode.

Thank you for always keeping me encouraged, inspired, and confident in my gift.

Introduction

Random thoughts often flood my mind sporadically, the moment my roosters' crowing begins to echo throughout the walls of my house. The roosters prompt the constant pacing of the lions and wolves that share the same space. Yes, Yes, I know some would question exactly where it is that I live, where roosters, lions, and wolves live in harmony. Well, it is actually a quaint three-level home in the middle of suburbia and the city, separated by an invisible border—and an intersection. My roosters are actually two feisty parakeets that reside in a cage above ground level, away from the three rambunctious kittens and two overbearing, protective dogs.

I begin my daily routine pouring kibbles and seeds into several food bowls, refreshing the aqua supply for all to share, and then I head for the basement to open the back door for the wolves to relieve themselves. I do all of these tasks before I attempt to whisper good morning into the ears of the mini human that hasn't begun to show any physical facial features, proving that I actually birthed him; internally, he's my identical twin if personality, attitude, and characteristics were analyzed for DNA.

My daily routine constantly reinvents my outlook on life, as I prepare to face a new day—because humans and animals are intriguing beings that leave a lot of random thoughts to be captured. Whether I am preparing a meal for my family, transporting my *"mini me"* to and from school, feeding the birds, walking the dogs, or cleaning out litter boxes, my mind often ponders away at random thoughts or questions. Thoughts or questions flow through my mind like: "Do birds ever get tired of standing on their perch, and if so, do they lean up against the cage?" or "Why do people in general find it awkward to tell someone they have a booger hanging in full frontal view, waving hello?"

I found my notepad quickly filling with comedic views, rants, and sometimes serious observations that left an imprint on my heart to remember for good ol' times. So I began to write mini stories reflective of the experiences, which constantly made my friends laugh or cry when I shared these thoughts—inspiring me to first begin to blog online.

These random thoughts and sometimes funny observations are just that—and hopefully you will get a good laugh, maybe experience an *Ah- Ha!* or *Girl, I've been there too moment.*

I hope these excerpts give women a chance to stop, observe and enjoy life—possibly identify with similar or identical circumstances. I am convinced that all women have experienced the same issues—perhaps during different intervals in life, or at least know someone that has traveled down similar paths in the crazy mini stories that you'll read.

My goal is to connect with other women by sharing my stories and possibly sparking a grin or a *pee in your pants* moment. Just enjoy my thoughts and reflect on your own experiences with the people in your lives that bring you love and laughter.

Random thoughts...that make you go HMMM!!

Day 1:

The Autobiography of Jahzara

Birthed into a world of chaos, my spirit rose from the womb and hovered with the angels until breath was digested into my lungs—then the bells rang loudly, announcing the arrival of a beauty . . . Me!

I'm that chick, moisturized with confidence, resilience, power, and faith, built to outlast the toughest circumstances often created to block my predetermined destiny.

Often, I'm like a raging bull, fearless and strapped with focus and determination ringing from the bells of my horns . . . my horns, locked and pointed directly at the haters of my world . . . the fake ONES who loosely use the terms love and friendship.

I'm pretty, yes, gorgeous indeed. I'm tagged with arrogance, conceit, but those who really know me can't deny that I'm a humble being that's sensitive as hell. Yes, I'm a sensitive chick flawed with the desire for perfection and straightforwardness with no chaser. I'm the lioness on the prowl to conquer success and will devour the naysayers who swallow double doses of the 40 oz gallon of HATERADE whenever I mention dreams and possibilities.

At night, I'm a *Tasmanian Angel* perched above ignorance and arrogance that fuel my intuitive side to rise above the mess. I rise above it all when I channel my supreme being who magnifies my true purpose. My destiny has been predetermined and is unchangeable. I am willed to speak my truths, which define me, but I am also funny, honest, strong minded, optimistic, and sensitive to lies and nonsense.

However, I can't be defined or labeled as normal or common. I'm tangled in a web of ordinary standards which my haters expect me to conform to their unwritten rules and guidelines, established by this fleshy world of chaos. Often times, I'm surrounded by conflict of which the socially brainwashed beings around me constantly try to socially hypnotize me into a socially induced coma . . . trying their best to define me as who they think I should be—traditional, tolerant, influenced, and gullible; everything and anything other than my true BEING.

I am Jahzara, the Savvy Diva. I'm a hometown city girl with a big, big, ego and a heart full of love. I love to talk and express my thoughts and opinions aloud, giving testimonial glimpses of my experiences and dysfunctional opinions. My humility is packed with a smile, sigh, or frown. Whether my days are long or my nights are short . . . I'm committed to communicating each and every thought.

Day 2:

She's Got a Big, Big, Alter . . . Ego

Five feet three inches tall, thick in the thighs, carrying the weight of a buck seventy-five (give or take); she's glazed with a caramel complexion and sits perched on her throne, staring at the world with her round apple eyes. I'm sure you've met her—she's swift with her comedic wit, and intuitively precise in detecting a potential harmful scene. Her name is KIKI, and she is the one who transforms from built-up anger. She's often summoned when her sweet lil' diva is unable to maintain poise and restraint when a violation occurs—just as lil' diva is backed into a tightly closed corner upon violation of her personal space zone. This zone is often scuffed and bruised by unsuspecting violators that may throw a word or two of insults, which dainty diva has no problem wiping nonchalantly off of her lil' dainty brow.

KIKI is the dainty diva's protector—the one that will pop up and stretch the weakened skin of the sweet, dainty diva's skeletal frame when she no longer possesses the small ounce of testosterone, that we (women) often keep clutched in our back pockets when the need to puff our chests out arises.

KIKI shows up, not as often as she did in my twenties, but often enough now in my thirties. She is my go-to *BITCH*. The one that I can depend on to say what I really wanted to say, but chose to keep pinned down in my politically correct, sometimes delayed mind. My delayed reactions are often due to sleep deprivation and uncontrollable ticks of emotions that overflow the moment that I get the hint that *Aunt Dot* is a few blocks away from ruining my last pair of sexy underwear.

KIKI always arrives the moment when I am burning up internally, and my face reddens with warning signs of a massive explosion. All the early signs are prevalent to the deserving jackass who just insists on pushing every last button on my "I'm not listening to your ass" panel. But suddenly, one of the buttons jams and I actually pay attention to the last word that floats sporadically past my ears, and then . . . I reach the point of no return. My nostrils flare, and my eyes flicker, and before the jackass can walk away, KIKI grabs the coattail and she's arrived to save the day.

KIKI's words begin to slice any eardrums in close range to her path and the ambience in the room has now become a self-esteem bloodbath. Her bionic strength often cleans plague off teeth, blackens eyes, and sometimes cures a slight nasal congestion. KIKI will sniff out every weakness on the deserving body and cut them down to a begging child seeking forgiveness. The deserving jackass that once stood tall while throwing insults now sits shamefully in a corner, speaking softly and seeking sympathy—as if his actions weren't the cause for the sudden cameo appearance.

When the shift ends and I mentally return, I am often in awe at the looks of shock and amazement of my hidden transformation. I am not always pleased with KIKI's whirlwind of chaos, because the casualties of her war often leave children that pass by in the midst of the transformation, afraid of KIKI's wrath– especially if they don't know what sent her ass flying in on her broomstick. I'm left with looking like the "*bad guy*" because no one really knows KIKI or believe that she really is me!

I'll just explain to the lil' ones who accidently catch a slight glimpse of KIKI's rants, that I was having a temper tantrum, and the fuel from my rants sparked fire from my tongue. That should hold them for at least a year—or until KIKI shows up again!

Day 3:

Balancing Acts

Extremists—That's how I define me and husband-to-be. I am the *spastic, time is crucial, let's go—let's do this, it's going to be now or never* chick, and he is *the tomorrow will take care of itself, there's no need to rush, let's just chill* type of dude. He's so laid back that if he were any more relaxed it would be impossible to distinguish him from a snail or a tortoise. He takes his time, observes a situation, researches possibilities, and then after maybe five years of thinking it over, he'll make a decision—but only after I've cornered him in a back alley with the heel of my three-inch stiletto pinching the nerves in his throat. I, on the other hand, make decisions based on my state of emotion and will deal with any repercussions that follow (maybe that's why I have a closet full of clothes and shoes that smell brand new). However, I possess great problem-solving skills, critical thinking skills, and an extreme sense of intuition—that has saved our lives on a daily basis. Come on, who wouldn't appreciate a girlfriend that had the courage of *Lassie*, and could detect danger and alert everyone to remove themselves from extreme conditions. *The love of my life*, on the other hand (let's call him *old man Sam*), is the guy Lassie finds sunbathing on the porch in his boxers (and no shirt) with a *Budweiser* in one hand and a *white boy* in the other. Lassie tries to alert that danger is approaching by bellowing out short, loud, pitched barks. Her provoking bark finally gets a rise out of *old man Sam's* intoxicated head after twenty minutes, only for her bark to be rejected by a rude and loud roar of "it's not that serious girl—get out of here."

I saved our lives one morning. We were resting comfortably in a hotel suite off the coast of the eastern shore, only to be awakened from a loud, roaring, noise followed by "THIS IS A FIRE ALARM—PLEASE EVACUATE THE BUILDING USING THE NEAREST EXITS AND USE ONLY THE STAIRS." So I did what any sane person who has experienced numerous fire drills at school and work would do, I jumped up, put on my pants, my jacket, and grabbed only the essential things that would be harder to replace— my purse with the car keys and wallet, etc. I cautiously headed to the door only to realize *the love of my life*, is rambling off scrambled words like,

"I thought I was in VIETNAM and we were under attack. Is the door open? I don't think it's in this hotel, I think it was a truck outside . . . wait, do you hear that, the truck just pulled off." WHAT THE HELL? I am starring at this patient man, loving his extreme side, and wondering, "Am I the crazy one?" So I instantly switched into critical thinking mode. I walked out into the hallway, just to see if I was the only crazy person on the floor, or if I'd be the only person standing outside of the possibly burning hotel—other than the army of firemen jumping off the five fire trucks I just spotted out of the hallway window. So, just as Lassie would've done, I ran back toward my hotel room door and thought maybe *the love of my life* was en route to meet me in the hallway. NOPE! *Old man Sam* was lying across the bed, with the phone receiver in one hand, and both feet dangling off the bed. It's weird, I don't know what made me notice the shadow of his dangling feet on the floor, but he was actually twirling his toes—which meant to me, he was pretty damn comfortable and not in a rush to find out if this was going to be our last day on earth. My panicky voice yelled at him to get up or be left, and then I asked who he was calling. Now hold fast to these words, he was calling the concierge. Again, WHAT THE HELL? He actually looked me in the eye and said, "The phone just keeps ringing, I wonder why no one is answering."

Seriously, what would you do? Would you agree that this was another moment for me to back him into a dark alley? Well that's the extreme measure I had to take. I had to tell him that the halls were packed with people fleeing for their lives, and that I overheard someone say that the flames were spreading fast from the top floors. *Old man Sam* pondered for a moment, because you know he has to assess the situation and then research the evidence. He concluded that he couldn't smell any smoke, which meant the fire wasn't that close to us, so we had a fair amount of time to depart. After several seconds of searching for his pants, shirt, and shoes—he felt the need to contemplate choosing either his fleece shirt or his jacket to wear on top of his T-shirt, since it may be a little nippy outside.

Finally, we were making good strides and we were headed away from danger. We decided to sit in our vehicle to keep our limbs warm, and waited patiently for the now one hundred and counting firemen to decide whether they were actually going to use the fire hose they pulled off the truck and put back on the truck, and then pulled off the truck again.

Fortunately for us, and the hotel, there wasn't a fire. Forty minutes later, we were shuffling through the hotel entrance loading onto the elevator to return to our room. A weird feeling came over me to check over *the love of my life*, and I suddenly noticed his untied shoestrings. Laid back *old man Sam* responded, "I had no time—there was no time, there was a fire."

You gotta love him . . . His laid back appeal and my *time is crucial* personality is the secret ingredient to complementing our extreme, yet balanced love.

Day 4:

If I Were a Boy . . .

The thought has crossed my mind multiple times on any given day, month, or when I'm having a blond moment at Jiffy Lube, Home Depot—even those hot ass days when the dress code should be shirtless. Now I will swear without hesitation that I am the strongest, bionic woman, that doesn't need to rely on anyone to do for me, what I can do for myself. I constantly find myself in physically compromising positions—like being pinned against my SUV and the shelving units in my garage because the truck was the perfect anchor to use all my weight to lift and then pull. The stories are endless when it comes to proving my physical capabilities, but the schizophrenic irony is, my proof is never in the pudding. My honey is always lecturing me about my need to impose self-inflicted challenges on myself that leave me whimpering my way into his massaging hands for comfort.

The only solution I can create to resolve my impatient flaws and chaotic urge to *"just do it"* is to just become a man-hero, in my own right. There are so many things I can probably achieve more successfully as a man—or at least try.

Picture it: If I were a boy—Every morning, I would wake up from a restful sleep, jump up out of bed unnerved, refreshed, and feeling pretty darn good about myself, my body, and most of all—my muscles, especially the strong one. Stretch first, pee straight with no spills, fart silently, scratch gently, and then flush. I'll let my lady sleep, wake up the kids, feed the cats, walk the dogs, drop the toast, spread the butter, pour the juice, fill the lunch boxes with all six food groups, stick a love note in between the juice boxes to say *I love you* . . . start the car, make the morning drop offs in record time; whistle and wink at the long-legged stilettos passing on the street, shift my manhood only three times throughout the day, stroke my beard only five—all before the strike of 9:00 a.m.

By early afternoon, I would've already paid my barber for a quick shape-up, shaven beard; already sped through the checkout lines of *Jiffy Lube*, *Lowes*, and *Sam's Club*; driven with my sunshades on grinning about the money I'd just saved on, tires, oil, brakes, hardware, tools, groceries, and beer. As the one o'clock hour ascended on the day, I would send my fifth "just thinking about you" text to my lady, I would crack open all twelve cans of beer, burp some, fart a lot, and pee in the backyard bushes as I began to work on my lady's household "to-do list"; check off the yard work, bag leaves, unclog bathroom sink, clean out old things, carry the thirty heavy boxes of random "*I don't know what this is used for*" things out of the shed.

The addictive urge to play a few games with the fellas on the *X-box 360* or *Playstation* consoles would consume my mind, as I tried to ignore the massive texts my entourage would continue to send in order to steal my mind—and then . . . I'd give in for more chicken wings and more beer. At the stroke of three o'clock, I'd call my lady for the fourth time, just to say hi. I would dial the cell phones of Mom or Dad to make sure they were sitting in the carpool line. I'd leave the fellas in the basement to finish my tasks, pay the household bills online before the creditors' deadlines. I would use the last two hours of my afternoon to install the new shelves in the garage to replace the shelving unit that my lady destroyed, re-pack the Christmas tree in a new storage bag I brought to replace the

one she tore when she attempted to lift and then
store—unsuccessfully.

As the day descends with the sun and the lanterns
on the street illuminate—I'd hasten my stance to
prepare for my queen's arrival. Suddenly, a miniature child appears yelling out words that my
tongue is used to projecting—"what's for dinner?"
DINNER—I'd then hesitate, noticing I have thirty
minutes to spare.

Forty-five minutes later, the queen arrives, and the
aroma of diligence and hard work fills the air, mois-
tening the palates of everyone's mouth as their
stomachs are filled with air. I would summon her to
sit as I pull tops off of the pots and pans—display-
ing my gift of a Chinese-themed dinner.

An hour later, my sweetie would begin to wipe her
mouth, stretch her back, and then exclaim out
loud her surprising satisfaction that her belly is full
and fat . . .

My sweetie would begin to clean up the kitchen
to balance the family tasks and suddenly she'd
appear in my view just as I gulp down two more
Budweisers. *Sweetie* leans in and thanks me for
helping her out, completing her lists, checking off
the items with only one miss . . . and before I attempt
to respond—she would reveal her discovery of the

Chinese restaurant take-out boxes that I forgot to throw away.

If I were a boy . . . at that moment I would wish I were a girl . . . so I would remember to pay attention to every detail.

Day 5:

Big, BiG, BIG—LOVE

Every January for the past four years, I've tuned into HBO to indulge in the season premiere of *BIG LOVE*. Each season is always filled with action-packed polygamy drama. The mere thought of tolerating a marriage shared by one man and his one, two, three—sometimes seven wives may or may not get a rise out of a few perfectly plucked arched brows.

I will admit, the first series premiere ignited emotions of "WTF"—"OMG" and "these people are in a cult"; especially when the first season ended around the time the feds raided the polygamy compound in Utah.

After the first episode, I was hooked. I surprised myself with intrigue when I thought how exciting it must be to live as the main characters in this drama.

Bill, the polygamy pimp, has his three chicas living in three separate single-family homes connected by one huge backyard. Life is grand for every-one, and he makes the money while the wives maintain the homes. The main wife, his legal wife, manages the everyday plural marriage nuances like scheduling nights of intimacy, alternating pregnancies, delegating tasks, running errands, managing budgets, distributing allowances, and paying bills. Most men would love this scenario, and I gotta admit I secretly love the distant, unre-alistic dream of the life they portray on screen.

Of course, I would have to be the head honcho in charge of that plural marriage. I need to control the environment of sharing my man, scheduling nights of intimacy, suppressing jealously, display-ing open-mindedness, and of course overseeing the unique sisterhood. Now, don't judge, I need you to really consider my thought process with this one. I only submerge my toes in this pool of multiple love and marriage for one selfish reason—to get some damn assistance. Everyone else can have personal assistants, why the hell can't I? It would really be beneficial for those of us who already run a household, maintain budgets, run errands, cook, clean, carpool, delegate responsibilities, and babysit our own kids—lol!

Seriously, wouldn't it be great if you could use the benefits of polygamy to benefit your life? I am not going to lie, there are those nights when wearing lingerie should be the only thing I'm concerned with to act grown and sexy for my *boo*, but the damn sandman is always at the edge of my lashes throwing buckets of sand in my lids. I would have to suck in and swallow the thought of sharing my man with other women. Perhaps they would only be scheduled to do certain things for him, and perhaps to carry a baby or two.

Just imagine—what if having a large family was the original goal set by you and hubby? Well, problem solved. You don't even have to keep stretching your body out of shape for his ass. You could just schedule one of those other sister bitches to do it for you.

I'm Just Saying, Man . . . having big, big, big, love for your man might not be that impossible!

Day 6:

Pet Peeves

Annoyances that seem minor can become a major factor of ruining my day. I often mouth these words in silence as random people, some-time family members or friends, violate the hidden law of my annoyance free zone. It can take the smallest gesture on someone else's part that will set off my radar—and suddenly my horns appear, my skin reddens, and splotches of inconvenience and annoyance are written all over my face.

I love the smell of anything that is fresh and new, especially if it is a magazine or book. I also love the subtle feeling of excitement that overcomes me when I'm tearing open a new CD or DVD.

Hopefully, it won't surprise you when I explain the sudden surge of rage I felt when I bought the newly released CD of my favorite songstress *Alicia Keys*. I was anxious to pay the cashier in Target so I could rush to my vehicle to rip open the plastic and pop in the CD. Well, my nephew accompanied me to the store, and while I was seeking my treasure, he reminded me that my mother requested a separate item that could be purchased only at the grocery store. I hastily walked to my vehicle to decrease the amount of time it would take to retrieve the grocery item and to listen to the melodic tunes of *Alicia Keys*. I rushed into the grocery store, and ten minutes later, returned in excitement, because nothing was going to stand in my way from tearing open my new CD. Hmmmm! I guess I should've made an announcement that the smudges on the plastic and CD case were going to come from only my fingers when I ripped open the case. I opened the door to my truck, and almost choked in anguish as I heard the familiar single track that had been playing on the radio for over three months. I sat down slowly in the driver's seat and ignored his compliments of the singer for the duration of our travels.

WTF . . . who the hell said it was ok to open my CD and listen to it without waiting for me? You can call me petty, but dang, I can't even make the claim that I was the first one to listen to THAT CD.

* * *

Of course, someone opening my fresh CDs isn't my only pet peeve. The other top peeve on my list is purchasing hot French fries exclusively for my fingertips to be burned upon impact. An order of hot fries and a milkshake is the best snack that doesn't make me feel guilty after I've been running errands on an empty stomach. If I'm in the car alone, the indulgence of that snack puts me in a trance as I am speeding through rush hour traffic. However, if I am not in the car alone—I will ask everyone as a courtesy if they would like to place an order when I pull up to the drive-through line. If my Aunt Alice is in the front seat with me, 99.9 percent of the time, her answer is always *NO*. Now I am never surprised, but I'm always screaming silently in my head when the drive-through teller hands me the bag of fries and chocolate milkshake. You see, just as I pull away from the window—guess whose hands are digging in the bag, pulling out a handful of piping hot, crispy salty fries. You guessed it, Aunt Alice. I just smile, as I have learned to prepare for the hidden answers of "I say no, but I really mean yes" responses; and just inform her that the box of fries on the top is just for her.

Again, WTF—Just say yes to the fries!

The petty annoyances are so small that the flaring of my nose and my squinting eyes are reactions to my pet peeves, which are discarded like gas or an upset stomach. One day I'll get up the nerve to let them know that violating things such as fresh CDs and hot fries bothers me—just as I hope others will realize that talking on cell phones at the checkout counter and leaving a sheet of toilet paper hanging from the roll to drag against the bacteria-infested bathroom floor are inconsiderate annoyances for others.

My list can go on for days about the irritating annoyances that gross me out, frustrate me, or just piss me off at the mere thought—so I will only consider creating a running list and updating my acquaintances to allay their thoughts that I am "just gassy with an upset stomach."

Day 7:

Cupcakes, Twinkies, and Wedgies

It was 9:30 a.m. and I was headed to my weekly staff meeting. The confidence and perkiness I exuded in the hallways were interrupted for the sixth time, as I had to slow my stride to dramatically step forcefully while shifting one butt cheek outward—hoping the sudden strut would allow the left side of my underwear to shimmy downward out of the foyer area of my butt. But no, I had to now take drastic measures with only two minutes to spare before I would be considered late.

So as a half-filled elevator opened in front of me and some people exited the elevator, I entered with a leap and threw myself into the back corner of the elevator—distracting those who stood with paranoia, trying to figure out what the hell was wrong with me. As everyone starred at each other and shrugged their shoulders with confusion, I used this window of opportunity to take action. I placed my hand behind my back, slid my right leg outward, pushed forward on my toes to increase my height and stuck the left side of my butt outward to give me the perfect angle to dig as quickly and as deep within the boundaries that my slacks would allow. With an ounce of time left floating in the air, I had a half a second left before the crazies in front of me would suddenly turn and stare at my distorted facial expression (*you know the look, when you tongue is externally positioned up toward the right side of your lip and your eyes are both turned inward*).

Successfully achieving the pinch-and-pull gesture, I prepared to exit the elevator feeling relieved and confident that my slacks no longer had a bulge of cotton lying over my right back pocket.

See, in that moment of inconvenience, I finally realized that perhaps my overindulgence of sweets on a daily basis was beginning to catch up with me. I couldn't believe that my once sexy underwear had become too small and were either going to cut off my circulation, or force me to wear *big girl drawers*. The weight began to form magnetic fields on my thighs during the winter months while the earth's atmosphere brewed inclement ingredients; producing blizzards, ice storms, and massive feet of snow, holding residents hostage for weeks at a time. Honestly, I really don't need a deadly storm to encourage my addiction to take over my flesh. The most beautiful day filled with blooming rosebuds and bright sunny skies will entice me to celebrate for that reason . . . sunny skies, and beautifully frosted cupcakes, cakes, and even cookies prompt me to fill my belly.

The mouth-watering crème cheese frosting mounted over five inches of devil's food cake sends my taste buds into crack-fend frenzies. Mmmm! On a daily basis I find it extremely hard to ignore the tiny voices inside my brain, that not only encourage me to purchase a twelve-pack of cupcakes from the bakery, that is conveniently located on the opposite side of the freeway from Wal-Mart, but also whispers commands to double-check the inventory of my deep freezer—just in case a storm is brewing.

My name is *Savvy*, I have a sweet tooth and I am a CHOC-A-HOLIC.

Day 8:

Bride-Polar

The old saying "always a bridesmaid and never a bride" rings loudly with equal bass, high volume of 100 and surround sound, in the ears of most women who receive the news that their best friend, cousin, sister—or even the girl at work who only speaks when it's work related—is getting *MARRIED*. But the moment you feel like you're close to becoming someone's fiancée, the mute button on your internal earphones permanently switches off.

Dating countless men to weed out the potential *Mr. Perfect* candidate is necessary, especially if you're on a timeline to complete your crazy, unrealistic *to do before age thirty list*. Of course practice makes perfect, and when you find the perfect guy that meets the criteria on your *Mr. Right's quality* list, you feel like the jackpot has your name on it. When Mr. Right becomes a constant, romantic force in your life for weeks, months, or one year—suddenly the eternal flame starts flickering and *Mr. Right* is now pegged to make you his wife. The thought just sends chills through my body, and ignites a flame in my heart, but I forgot to mention, *Mr. Right* didn't get the memo that you expect him to marry you within the next year.

Suddenly the occasional conversations about marriage, children, houses, and joint checking accounts become regular, daily conversations. You begin to purchase bridal magazines, and send sporadic e-mails to him with images of wedding bands, engagement rings, and jewelry store recommendations. The memo pads on your desk are stained with *Mrs. Right* (with and without a hyphen) to consider the alternative to maintaining your maiden name. Your obsession for bridal reality television shows raise a few eyebrows, but no one mentions any concern because of the visible daggers in your eyes.

You start dragging your mother out every weekend to attend local bridal expos that you've discovered in your daily bridal research frenzy, promising yourself and her that you're only going to go to local expos. Suddenly every weekend in February and March you leave home to venture farther and farther outside of the hour minimum ride restriction stamped on your research crazi-ness. Your evenings are filled with sifting through the expo bags of brochures, buttons, coupons, business cards, and yes, memorabilia that proves you've attended one too many expos—especially when your *future fiancé* is constantly scratching his head questioning why you're even attending bridal shows. The final straw is plucked when you miraculously pick the winning ticket for the free bridal gown raffle. You race home in excitement to tell your *almost fiancé* of the inevitable experi-ence, but overlook the blank stare he repels that should've screamed clues that he's lingering on chapter three of the relationship, and you're three hundred pages ahead.

Two weeks later, you're standing on the circu-lar carpeted platform surrounded by mirrors that reflect a beautiful bride. A *perfect fit* for the *perfect wedding* uniting you with the *perfect man* secretes across your lips into the air, solidifying the symbol-ism of being blessed with a free wedding gown—and nearly completing your wedding checklist. One last stop—find the perfect wedding venue. Readers, please take your positions now. A disaster is brewing at a fast point of no return. Whether it is your best friend, daughter, cousin, or sister—you are morally obligated to shake the shit out of her at this point. Speak to her with audio output of 500 to override the permanent mute on her internal earphones. Let her know the man must propose first. The last thing you should do is give her space, allowing her to sign a contract for a wedding venue, with a faux date, and a hidden proposal. Your loved one is borderline crazy, and her actions warrant a cussing out.

But what really defines crazy? Perhaps optimism is the key element to rely on things falling into place. At least when he finally proposes, the planning process will be complete and the wedding will be the final chapter. It's your choice; let her ass worry you now, or wait until *Mr. Right* actually fast forwards to the last few chapters in *almost Mrs. Right's* book, and he realizes he's a main character in her *almost wedding* fantasy.

Day 9:

Never Leave Home Without 'em

There are many elements that are key compo-
nents to my morning ritual; the warm greeting of
the sun kissing my cheek, or the sound of purring
cats vibrating my inner ear to alert me that not
only is it morning, but it's time for them to eat. It's
a chain reaction of rituals that leads into the dogs
barking and the kid waking up demanding a full
course breakfast. The ritual is so seamless that I
could complete it in my sleep. After I complete
the latter, I prepare to dress myself and the kid,
which is normally successful . . . unless there is a
wardrobe change request because the kid is so
particular about the shirts I choose for him to wear.
Normally I have minutes to spare—on a good

day—and I'm often patting myself on the back for another successful morning without chaos.

Everyone's loaded in the car, seatbelts are securely buckled, and the rpm quickly increases to 200. The morning is fantastic. So I think. It's only when I'm about eight blocks away from the house that I realize I forgot the one thing that makes me feel whole—my *eyebrows*. I suddenly become insecure and panicked. The thought of having a naked face prompts the acidic juices in my stomach to turn at the speed of a spin cycle. My natural eyebrows are so thin and fine, so I use a brow pencil that enhances them, which leaves me looking more beautiful than ever. I actually sound like a commercial.

My eyes start bulging outward, I start scratching my head, I turn my neck left—then right. My mind is stuck and I can't spark my brain to flash images of the location of my new brow pencil. Did I put it in my purse when I decided to change bags in the foyer this morning? Think—think! My mind is stuck. I have to act fast and make an executive decision. Should I turn around and go through eight blocks of traffic lights and bumper-to-bumper cars to boost my self-esteem, or stay on course and get the kid to school on time?

Seriously, what would you do?

I come to a traffic light that allows me at least a minute to grab my purse and dump out all the contents. No pencil or a trace of pencil shavings in the bottom of the makeup bag. Now is the time to decide the fate of my face or my son's education. So I did what any loving parent would do. I rummaged through my purse in search for my notebook, scribbled a late arrival excuse note for my son and made a U-turn to head for my house. Ten minutes later, I'm standing in my basement bathroom enhancing my look and accessorizing my face.

An hour later, I pull onto the campus parking lot of my son's school. My son has no clue about his tardiness or my naked face. He is just excited that he has a few extra minutes to take a catnap and play extra rounds on his *Nintendo DS*. We enter the doors to the school with our heads held high and I kiss my sweet prince good-bye, whispering in his ears, "Have a productive day, my love—because Mommy will now do the same."

Seriously, what would you do?

Day 10:

Lunchtime Memories

I remember the daily lunchtime march toward our school's multipurpose room that mysteriously transformed every day into our lunch cafeteria by the stroke of 11:30a.m. My kindergarten class marched in unison with the first graders in a single formation, as if we were militant soldiers breaking for chow time. In perfect strides, the soles of our loafers and black and white tie-up shoes rustled through the reddish orange leaves that outlined the direct path to lunchtime heaven. The squeaking of metal lunchboxes painted with cartoon legends like Wonder Woman, Spiderman, Popeye, and the Smurfs, drowned out the subtle crackling of the limited hand-carried paper brown-bagged lunches.

The squeaking chipmunk voices outside the multipurpose room alerted the lunchroom monitors that the lower class militia had arrived. Suddenly, the dragging and vibrating scrapes of metal chairs being extracted away from the wood-topped tables signaled the ringing of brass-covered bells, cueing the militia to regain order and silence. One last bellow of brass ringing bells chanted in our tiny ears, giving us the green light to begin consumption of our daily bread.

A high-fashioned buffet of rainbow-bright sandwiches slowly revealed mouth-watering morsels of pleasure, yet sometimes the unleashed smell of rotten egg salad sandwiches would trigger gag reflexes. However, my lunch as a child brought pleasure to my ravenous palate, and often prompted others to whisper deals of exchange and trial periods—but the delectable treasures were exclusive to me. I adored the double mounted slab of apple butter equally glazed across two toasted slices of Sunbeam squares; squished between a brown striped yellow banana and a yellow thermos filled to capacity with strawberry Kool-Aid, laced with powdered mix around the brim. The perfect ending to this memorable lunch was the sweet indulgence of my favorite Hostess Susie Q cake. My belly tingled with satisfaction from the mountain peaks of sugary vanilla icing that triggered memories of pure enjoyment of lunch as a child.

Day 11:

I Love Me Some HIM . . .

I'm dangerously in love with HIM. He's the man of my dreams, the hero in my life, the rhythm and rhyme to my poetic heart. The flame I hold for him is so dangerous, it makes my heart skip several beats in one interval cycle, pumping blood through my veins—my internal core. I hope you've experienced a great love such as mine, but if you haven't, here is a taste.

Imagine an emotion-filled basket full of favors that ignite summer breezes of passion, lust, infatuation, admiration, motivation, dedication, and commitment—topped with warm fuzzy variations of sweet cinnamon, nutmeg, and chocolate-dipped strawberries and whipped cream. Now imagine an unlimited supply of these delectable variations reproducing upon consumption at unimaginable speeds, even through unpredictable storms, tornadoes and hurricanes of life. My love for HIM exceeds infinity; exuberant, sparkling diamond-covered butterflies fill in my belly and increase in numbers with each year, month, day, kiss; each stroke of my face, the bare touch of our skin, gentle hugs, nighttime cuddles, and grown and sexy moments.

At first glance, you'll be intimidated by his no-nonsense credibility that forces street thugs and *Corporate America* to bow down with respect in his presence. My love for him inspires me to be dedicated to family, committed to my faith, and I seek the same fuel that ignites him to be purposeful and responsible.

My HIM is the calm to my chaos. His ability to reason and resolve often forces my independence to bow off stage and submit to a role of the damsel in distress. His voice arouses the hidden mischievous child in me that seeks discipline with authority. His walk is cool but rugged and his swag is mild and authentic, which forces a steady focus on the mystery behind the strength and agility carried in his legs. The seductive eyes on my man stare out the secrets to every warm nook and cranny of my being. The care label to his soul is revealed only to those who are as lucky as I am, to exist in the same space and close enough to sneak a peek at each layer of his core. The passion I have for HIM is just as high now as it was when we first met—the days he called himself my "Clyde" and me, "Bonnie, his ride or die chick." That dangerous chick still exists, and her craziness is even more prevalent, yet remains abundantly pure—but the purity can easily be altered, leaving me in a trance to break down any bitch that dares to test my commitment to our dangerous love.

He's my rock, my wind, my trees, and he makes me smile for eternity. My HIM, dispels all the myths that *Good Guys* don't exist. Well my HIM is a good guy and his tender soul and warm heart won my heart for life.

I love me some HIM, he's my best friend and my King.

Day 12:

Fifty Feet Please!

Abiding the laws of personal space should be a requirement for every U.S. citizen. Seriously, how many times have you stood in the checkout line and felt someone breathing on your neck? Lately, I've found myself mouthing the words, "Fifty feet please!" as I stand in line waiting to use the ATM or in a bank line waiting for my turn to extract funds. What is wrong with people who feel it's their natural born right to stand so close to you to enable them to read every word on your personal identification card?

Now I don't have high blood pressure, but I think I've actually felt the systolic and diastolic numbers rise and fall a few times while standing in line. The potential release of my untamed tongue destroying the boring ambiance in the pharmacy increases when the silent prayers are no longer able to keep my raging thoughts contained. The heels of my feet aren't equipped with skid-resistant shields and I'm not OK with leaving out of the store with Band-Aids covering the scrapes on my heels from the ten close encounters between the lil' lady behind me and my vulnerable heels. If I knew I was going to be in line in front of this hardcore chick, I wouldn't have worn sling-backs. I first thought her motive was to injure me, but then I began to think she may have a case of Alzheimer's and thought she accompanied me to the store to purchase her prescription. Hell, I thought about going along with that craziness if that would guarantee she would sit down and wait for me to pay at the counter. Just as I lose the last ounce of patience because prayer could no longer help succumb the urge of scaring the crap out of the fragile soul by unleashing my tongue to dispel forceful chants that would encourage her to back the hell up—the cashier motions for me to approach her at the register.

My favorite close encounters are moments in the grocery store self-checkout lines. There is an invisible force that overpowers the minds of shoppers, enticing them to stand and witness your art of scanning groceries. They watch every move you make with amazement as you weigh your own produce and vegetables, and get even more excited as you scan your milk, eggs, ice cream, and butter. Suddenly they become more intense in their task of observation when you lean toward the screen to key in the total number of muffins or donuts in the pastry bag; as if they have been temporarily employed to monitor your transactions. I crack up as I ask them for assistance in bagging my items—since they want to be a part of my shopping experience.

Personal space violators are just too damn close for my comfort. I have the perfect remedy for the awkward space invaders. I encourage anyone who feels a violation of personal space has occurred in a checkout line to implement the following: turn slowly without warning and face the violator, smile and look straight ahead with your hands folded, and blurt out random chants of impatience for long lines and close encounters. I guarantee your personal space will be granted instantly.

Day 13:

The Sky is Falling . . .

The familiar words "hit, rock and bottom," often associated with bad times and people who do bad things, buzzed passed my mind one sweltering summer afternoon. I felt like an addict walking into my first anonymous meeting, raising my hand to attest to an awakening. I can picture myself standing up very slowly, attempting to delay the squeaking noise of the crooked ass chair that supported my tired ass ten seconds prior to my revelation to stand and testify. Again, I picture myself clearing my throat. I prepare my words to proclaim that I often find myself feeling like I'm in the midst of climbing a mountain. With each attempt to plant the sole of my Timberland boot into the nooks and precisely cracked earth—it crumbles beneath me. I sigh deeply as I scan the room for sympathy or at least a head nod of confirmation that the experience is symbolic to a change occurring in my life. Fortunately for me, I'm not in an anonymous meeting, but sadly, I am being smacked out of a walking coma of false reality, by a rejuvenating bolt of lightning.

Screams awaken my unintentional sleep and more screams calm me. I yell loudly into the air to acknowledge those who wonder why they haven't heard from me in months, (but haven't reached out to discover why they haven't received my daily, weekly, or monthly "just checking on you" calls). ATTENTION, ATTENTION. If you were wondering, I've hit rock bottom. Now get your minds out the gutter—I am not in that bottomless, crack-infested pit overflowing with Patron, Ciroc, or Courvoisier. No, I'm in a pit covered with huge boulders, creek rocks, and heavy ass paper weights surrounded by three months of bills, depleted credit scores, overdrawn bank accounts, bare cupboards, pantries, freezers, empty ass gas tanks, and the burden of relying on family to stimulate my financial state to avoid drowning.

The interesting thing I've discovered is, with all of this weight I'm carrying, I can attest to being blessed. I have the option to turn to my mother for financial support, and to live in a house that protects my son and me from cruelty that exists beyond my front door. I thank the Lord, my heavenly father, for every blessing he bestows upon me. It's my faith that keeps me strong enough to carry the weight of the rocks that exceed my height.

. . . But I'm also human. I also become weak in the midnight hour, gasping for air when my burdens are too much for me to endure. My head sinks under the thrashing water and the shores of optimism and strength to overcome are nowhere in sight.

Suddenly a friendly hush overwhelms my spirit, and I open my bible, just as the sun kisses the moon— "Good morning. Goodnight." I become fixated on the book of Psalms -69:1-4,

"Save me O' God, for the waters have come up to my neck. I sink in the mere depths where there is no foothold."

Scriptures bring me comfort and restore my faith, allowing me to face another day . . . even when the sky is FALLING!

Day 14:

The Sole of a Woman

The subtle scraps of stiletto heels or just two-inch pumps echoing against the cemented sidewalks can be observed on any city block. Women love shoes and many of us share the common gift of an abundance of shoes spilling out of our closets. But have you ever wondered about the lives of the women that wear these sought-out accessories?

At first glance, whether it's a first encounter or a daily acquaintance, I look at the shoes on a person's feet. It's a serious obsession, but someone has to police the situation. It seems people are always looking to judge a person by their exterior, and I think shoes are the perfect platform to base the superficial rating.

Now don't mistake me for being shallow—because I'm definitely familiar with the old saying, "You can't judge a book by its cover." However, when you're used to seeing the *marketing chick* in your department at work wear three- and four-inch pointy stilettos, platform pumps, and sandals to work for the past three years, your mind would spiral in a tail spin when she rushes into the staff meeting wearing slightly oversized, fat, distressed, round top brown calf boots that need a serious polish job. Of course no one noticed the relapse except for me, and the expression on her face lead me to assume there was a hidden story behind the change of fashion. Fortunately in this instance, her income wasn't slighted and the setback was temporary. After the staff meeting ended, she felt compelled to explain her sudden interest in the new flatware that enveloped her small size six feet. Though I made it clear an explanation wasn't necessary, I certainly wasn't going to pass up the voluntary spill of information.

Apparently, in her morning commute, she decided to stop by her neighborhood shoe repair shop to have the heel on her favorite "everyday work stiletto" repaired, because she tripped over a steel grate on the street and her heel was snatched off. Unfortunately for her, the time it would take to repair her heel would exceed the spare time she had before her presence would be missed in the mandatory staff meeting. So since the *marketing chick's* time was limited, they sent her on her way with a random pair of boots that hadn't been picked up by the owner for over four months.

This bizarre story prompted me to question the real stories behind the shoe choices that violated my fashion dos and don'ts. The *marketing chick's* morning of inconvenience could've led many to wonder whether a life-altering experience altered her normal choice of footwear. Whether it was the economy, an orthopedic mandate for her to avoid high heels, or an unpreventable accident on the street during the normal hustle and bustle to work during rush hour, the sole of this woman's choice was questioned for a split second.

I've vowed to observe and no longer make assumptions about women wearing shoes that may be tethered, torn, ripped, scuffed, or secretly glued at the seams. There may be real tragedies, sacrifices, and economic choices behind the footwear—or perhaps they've experienced a sidewalk shoe fatality.

Day 15:

I Remember When . . .

Reminiscent days fill my brain, leaving no room in my gray hard drive for present day thoughts.

Life has become so stressful that my mind switches to auto run. You know, the mode of self-defense and survival. The overwhelming flood of everyday stresses triggers the auto reboot switch to pop onto Hemisphere Avenue, located south of the skeletal cavity. It's the moment when your body temperature rises rapidly from the lack of flowing air you'd wish you were receiving from the hand-me-down oscillating fan on the hottest summer night. The only air you manage to catch is the semi-cool breeze circulating past the window every ten minutes. Every nagging fly, gnat, or mosquito buzzing past your ear convinces you the darkness gets thicker by the minute.

Electrical sparks flicker throughout my frontal cavity, and my body begins to protect me from the surrounding enemies. I become numb and the hairs on my neck and arms stand at attention. Colorful, florescent lights illuminate the streets and familiar neighborhoods lead me toward familiar houses of laughter, adventure, and memorable experiences. The streets are covered with chocolate and every front door is wide open, enticing me with waving hands, percolating music, delicious-smelling food and billboards listing the featured memories playing at each house. So many featured playbacks to choose from, it would take days, weeks, or even months to enjoy. Memories of first kisses, first crushes, first dates, first loves, boyfriends, best friends, parties, shopping, sweet sixteen, a license to drive, first car, legal twenty-one, drinking, more parties—countless mornings and afternoons of sleeping in to recover from drunken parties; weekend getaways, diva trips, first new car, first new home, first real job, pregnancy, firstborn, then suddenly the memories freeze. The music stops abruptly, the doors to the familiar houses shut and then pure-white sterile lights shine bright.

My eyelids begin to flicker rapidly and my ears start ringing from the overload of words tailgating at the entrance of my outer ear canal, causing a massive pile up of information. My brain begins spinning like a windmill downloading the messages received . . . and then my eyes begin to focus in on the images standing before me. I decipher the last three words that made it through my inner ear, "Mommy, do you remember when?"

Day 16:

What's in Your Wallet?

The variety of wallets clutched in the hands of shoppers often catches my eye, which signals random questions to explode in my mind, like "What's in your wallet?" I've often stood behind someone in the checkout line of Target, Wal-Mart, or the grocery store, and quickly glanced over at a wallet being thrown on top of the metal counter by its owner, as the poorly manicured fingers sift through the wallet's interior compartments, seeking some type of monetary currency in exchange for the items on the belt. Now I am not usually a nosy person, but if the person is standing close enough for this observation, I will take a few minutes to waste my energy and pay attention to these random things.

I've seen people carry wallets that hold three Visas on one row and an American Express or Discover on the next row. My first impression is the person likes to shop, has a job, probably a high credit score, and mostly uses credit cards for everyday purchases. To my nosy and judgmental surprise, the shopper pulls back the hidden sleeve inside the wallet and reveals a wad of bills, totaling $150.

Now, if someone were as nosy as me with a few minutes to spare while the customer in front of her was unloading a cart full of unnecessary items— only to disrupt the cashier's flow of scanning to demand a price check on already marked-down items, that first glance of my wallet would reveal STRUGGLE all over the front flap. First of all, the person would witness me implement my infamous process of elimination of three maxed-out Visas, one MasterCard, and two Visa check cards, which keep sending DECLINED messages.

The inside zipper of my wallet also holds a few random pieces of lint, folded motivational readings that are faded and smudged from the residue of my fingertips constantly unfolding to read, reflect, and reboot. My outlook on life, liberty, and the pursuit of cashing in on a lottery ticket that displays numbers I dream about and numbers I pray will appear on the white ball during the evening lotto drawing. I can dream elaborate dreams, apparently that's the only thing I do well—along with collecting enough change to fill the mini pocket section that is often weighed down by an abundance of pennies and nickels.

I utilize every pocket and zipper section, of my wallet. So those who glance over my shoulder, seeking enough data to reach a conclusion of what type of person I am by the contents of my wallet—don't bother, just call me resourceful. I'm not rich, but I want to be. I carry unnecessary things every day to remind me of my past mistakes. Reminiscing on my poor decisions helps me stay focused on future goals and plans.

So when I open my wallet and glance at the old receipts for clothes that I never wore and see maxed-out credit cards that can't even help me purchase gas, I stay focused and purchase only items that will override the struggle on the front flap of my wallet with the words...SUSTAIN ME.

Day 17:

Jealously

If you haven't realized by now, Jealousy is universal and it is definitely universal among the female gender. I have experienced dozens of jealousy issues with my girlfriends, and surely it doesn't discriminate with age.

You think after you've stormed through the high school and college years, you no longer have to worry yourself with thoughts of your best friend having other friends. Bringing a new person into the group or spending more time with one friend is OK, right? Wrong! The thought of bringing someone new into your circle of tightly knit friends doesn't calculate into the equation for some women. The most unforeseen jealous rages hurdle many obstacles in between the best friendships, and many ask the question, "Why can't we all just get along?"

Don't lose sleep over this epidemic, because no matter what role you play in these relationships, human nature will never change. However, I do have a slight theory. The one unique characteristic women possess is the ability to nurture. Women invest so much energy and focus on relationships. So any posed threat, especially the threat of another woman ('cause all women can be catty and possessive) embarking on marked territory will send the brain electrical shocks to jumpstart the overload of jealousy.

Now personally, I can't say I've had an emotional overload since 2001, but will defend those who are six months shy of age thirty and have not chosen to take the non-jealousy pill. Why should we bow down to the new kid on the block, when we've spent countless hours passing Kleenex and listening to our best friend sob over spilled milk—I mean Rick!

So, Ladies, I say bow down with pride, and then vow to never give into jealousy—unless it's embarking on the territory of your man!

Day 18:

Less than Perfect!

Enough is enough, when will it end? The day to day addictive activity of rushing home through gridlock traffic only to find yourself in front of that big fifty-two-inch flat screen television (that you begged your boyfriend to get, baiting him with the reward of seeing his PlayStation games much clearer) just to catch the newest episode of the reality shows, I call unrealistic.

Why do we feel compelled to become enthralled in this hype? What's missing from our lives? Do we enjoy watching other individuals as they display *less than perfect lives?*

Just think about it. A woman enters a crowded room with her head held high, propelling her confidence from her fragranced skin. Women who are less than confident about themselves will find a reason to talk negative about this woman, noticing every loose piece of thread from her dress; the shredded lines in her stockings and the unnoticeable lean of her three-inch, run-down, stiletto heel. See, I am smiling and nodding my head as I write this. Until now, I never thought about the real deep, dark, hidden insecurities that motivate our actions. Now I've been on both sides of the fence. I've been the snickering woman surrounded by other insecure women, commenting on everything about the other woman. Yet, I've also been the woman who entered the room very confident and secure in my own skin. Both sides of the fence made me feel insecure after being in both environments. The insecure side of me couldn't decipher why insecurity plagued my mind so viciously and the confident me, wondered why strangers or acquaintances disperse so much animosity for me.

The women who enjoy snickering about torn stockings and run-over heels are the ones who can't enjoy life without laughing at others. So maybe reality shows were created for the snickering souls and its successful growth is just a mere glimpse of how many *less than perfect* addicts are actually watching . . .

Day 19:

Dressing for Success

Fashion mishaps during post engagement are highly usual, especially if you have birthed a child, maintained a passionate romance, all while trying to lock down a designated matrimony date. Well, no one told me that the desire to look and feel sexy would be thrown out the window once you have spent more than 2,880 days with the man you plan to spend every waking moment with.

Yes, Yes, I am prissy to some extent. I love dressing up or dressing down, as long as the outfit is cute. Every morning I spend about thirty minutes perfecting my hair, eyebrows, and eye shadow (because your eyes reveal truth). Then I spend another thirty minutes figuring out what outfit, shoes, and earrings I should wear. After a full hour of glamour rituals, I rush out in a mad dash to work for eight hours with folks who probably couldn't care less about my cute outfit, let alone me.

Outfits, shoes, etc. all of the prep time to display these articles leads me to this question: *Why do we dress for success professionally but not personally?*

In lieu of searching for the answer, this is all I could decipher. We let down our guard to those closest to us, which brings about comfort, and amnesia. I remember the beginning phases of my relationship I felt butterflies fluttering continuously in my stomach at the thought of seeing the love of my life, pondering for hours on what I would wear when I saw him. Now, I tie my scarf on my head before bedtime ('cause that's what most women of color throw on their heads to protect their hair at night) and a T-shirt and socks. The love of my life often poses the question, "what happened to that nightgown I brought you for Christmas last year?" I thought about his question the other night, as we were hanging around the house, feeling comfortable—and thought maybe I should reassess my actions and make my relationship successful.

Ladies, let's stop wasting that hour worrying about how we look for the professional world if we aren't using an extra hour in the evening to beautify ourselves later for our men. We need to be successful personally first, and then professionally.

Day 20:

A Uniformed Society

If we drive the same car, wear the same clothes, and date the same type of man, our world would be a safer place—you think?

Sometimes I wonder if the world functioned on one set standard, the thought of *keeping up with the Joneses* would never cross our minds. I'll even be the first to admit that I would probably never think about what I didn't have or wanted if the person driving next to me didn't drive a bigger truck, and the woman three doors down from my house didn't grow greener grass. People are never satisfied with what they have, so we build our hopes and dreams on striving to get the same purse, watch, and car as the person sitting next to us.

Those who can't afford buying the exact object will then turn to the derogative mentality, "I want it so I'll take it," which leads to the inflation of crime in our neighborhoods, schools—the whole world. If we didn't live in a creative world that is constantly reinventing the same products giving you different varieties, we would definitely have fewer choices to make. Besides, how frustrating is it to have to choose between twenty different cell phones with thirty-five unique options that allow you to choose from hundreds of downloadable ring tones?

A reduction in choices will reduce the urge to take what someone else has and others can't afford. Crime rates will drop in all neighborhoods because everyone will own the same house, with the same wall colors, furniture, and electronics. This will bring more unity in the communities and everyone will engage in conversation more as they enjoy life more—plus, there will be a Pottery Barn in the nucleus of every neighborhood!

You see, bad guys will avoid anything that doesn't stand out. I can be optimistic and dream unrealistically—can't I?

Day 21:

Bread Crumbs and Humble Pie

RECESSION, POVERTY—Two bold, rambunctious words swirling around in my brain as I attempt to rationalize the depletion of fluid funds in all of my accounts. Both checking accounts and both my savings, all hit less than $100. Damn... how did I get here? Its official, my financial situation has decreased in fewer than thirty days. Ah, yes, I can almost smell the scent of forest green bills igniting in my wallet. Sixty days ago, I had four major credit cards that had limits exceeding $5,000, and as soon as I denounce my single life, irresponsible thinking, and useless spending, I get smacked with the biggest sucker punch of my thirty-something life.

It all started when I decided to unite with *Team Marital Bliss*. You know, the team that does everything together—from budgeting, balancing checkbooks (in my case, reviewing all my receipts folded up in an envelope that I refer to as the overflow file, once my wallet's zipper begins popping at the seam), and checking off to-do lists that we've comprised as one unit. I sometimes think back to jolt my memory to see if I saw this behavior as a tip from a "Building Your Nest" segment on *Rachael Ray* or *Martha Stewart*. Someone had to tip me off, because this was soooo not the way I remember living or existing. Now *Team Marital Bliss* is really a great team to reside on, but I sometimes long for the days of my past life when I would walk into let's say, *New York & Company* and whip out my sleek black store credit card and charge about $500 on the latest cropped pants, tunics, jeans, belts. Now I feel repulsed by the mere fact that every other clothing rack in the store resembles the clothes hanging in my closet. Oh, but wait, it's just as sickening when I realize I'm standing next to my twin—the mannequin wearing the exact black knit dress and crimson red cardigan. The only way you can tell us apart is that she's wearing New York & Company shoes and I am rocking my black BCBG Girls pumps with a cute lil' bow. Those were the reckless days of my life, when the only excitement that filled me was spending money on clothes, shoes, or purses.

So here I am, almost twenty-four months, seven days, and three hours, from the last time I splurged on a pair of shoes or random clothes without feeling guilty or even thinking about *Team Marital Bliss*. Soon as I agreed to be responsible, all my credit cards were unavailable—you know, like me, unavailable from the dating scene and the single life of mingling, drinking, and partying. A life I voluntarily gave up, and have no regrets, but Damn, Damn, Damn . . . did I have to give up my credit cards and my unlimited spending habits? I actually feel like *Florida Evans* from *Good Times*. I'm counting pennies, clipping coupons, and praying *James Evans* will make it another day without being laid off from his job.

Last week I drove to Sam's Club to grab a few required items that the household needed—some chicken, wheat bread, etc. I was standing in the checkout line praying for a miracle that my check card transaction would be approved because I wasn't really confident it would approve my request to feed my family. The cashier looks at me with disappointment (as if I have ruined her day) and whispers to me that it was DECLINED. I held my head up high, and told her I would scurry over to the ATM and return once I retrieved some cash. I knew I was fibbing, and so did she, but I still scurried with confidence only to realize that the cashier and all of the customers in the line watched my every move at the ATM. Damn, Damn, Damn, I don't even have a lot in the cart. I just need a lil' bit of breadcrumbs to curve our hunger. Feeling defeated after receiving three receipts stating INSUFFICIENT FUNDS, I walked in haste with my head held high to tell the cashier that I've forgotten my pin number and turned and walked out of the store never looking back.

I recovered quickly after tossing back two bottles of *Moscato* later that evening—don't judge! The pain of embarrassment was hidden temporarily because two days later, I found myself sitting in my truck laughing hysterically after experiencing another case of checkout line embarrassment in Children's Place. This time, the purchase was for my son because he needed a pair of dress pants and lucky for my budget, the pants were on sale. Even though I had $20 dollars in my wallet, I chose to whip out my Children's Place card for a $14.99 purchase, so I could benefit from my 10% member discount—since my card displays the discount sticker. Of course it was declined, because I forgot to pay my bill, but this time, the clerk wasn't so discreet. She announced this issue to the whole store, but I remained calm, smiled continuously all the while, calling her a ton of "ghetto ass bitches" in my head, whispering to myself—"remain humble; the victory will be so sweet."

I ended up purchasing the pants with the $20 dollars I had in my wallet, and found myself ten minutes later clutching my coupon book in the parking lot of my neighborhood grocery store. I began praying that I would figure out how the family could eat that night because I hadn't had a chance to grocery shop for a couple of weeks, and wasn't sure how far the $4.30 I had left in my wallet could really take me. I found coupons for lunchmeat, Capri Sun juices, a loaf of bread, and a Popeye's chicken coupon. I took a deep breath and approached the line, and to my surprise, the woman who gave me life was standing in front of me . . . sweet, sweet, MOMMY!

Prayer is good, and humble hearts really do get far. That night, I was able to get the groceries I had in my cart, plus a box of chicken, biscuits, and a lil' pie on the side!

Day 22:

Lions, Tigers, Bears, Spirits . . . Oh My!

What really goes on while we're sleeping? I often ponder that question, seeking a logical explanation, as I rise from my slumber with the sun after a sleepless night. I recap the previous night and analyze all the activities that led to the exhaustion seeping out of the pores of my body. The flickering lights of the television and cupful of sand that the *Sandman* poured into my eyes are the only recollections that cross my sleepy mind, until I look downward at my twisted feet entangled in the sheets. My memory is ignited as I remember the three instances throughout the night when I awoke several times from my body tossing and turning continuously over my 100-thread count sheets—(yes, I know 100-thread count and not 300 count at least? It's a RECESSION!)

I remember instantly, my *SPIRIT* was in a spiritual battle throughout the midnight hours, protecting me from the lions, tigers, and beastly bears that enter the realms of our world, my home—my sanctuary. My *SPIRIT* hovers over my flesh every night as I sleep, camouflaged in all black, protecting me from every ill spirit that reeks of terror attempting to unleash a ball of destruction. I see why some nights my sleep is more intense and deep—the type of sleep where you can actually feel yourself waking up but something is preventing you from opening your eyes or even speaking. You feel your mouth moving and your heart rate intensifies as your body is weighed down by an indescribable power that isn't harmful, but protective. Those are the nights when my spirit has traveled further away from my flesh to battle distant forces that are light-years away from reaching my sanctuary.

Every night, from 2:30–4:00 a.m., I awaken instantly like clockwork—and though I am only awake for a few minutes, it is long enough to realize that something is different. My spirit takes flight from my flesh just as my mind enters the REM state of sleep. Into battle, she guards my soul, and throughout the attacks, she's feeding me internal ammunition to download when my flesh is active—just in case

I have to battle up when the moon fades away and the sun awakens.

So waking up in the morning from a restless night of sleep isn't hard on my body. See I forgot to mention—my face gleams bright, with a reflection of renewed strength sparkling in the corner of my eyes. I welcome those adventurous nights of tossing and turning—it's the morning that I wake up from a night of uninterrupted sleep that would concern me. I would wonder what really happened while I slept peacefully.

Day 23:

First Kiss, First Everything . . .

It starts with innocent glances, smiles, winks, friendly gestures, and, of course, the physical attraction sweetens each seductive thought. I can't speak for all, but I've held many conversations over fine wine and vodka with my girlfriends. We've discussed in detail the horrific memories of losing our virginities and the memorable moments of experiencing pure pleasure. Most of us agreed that our first intimate time, the destruction of the *Cherry*, was the #1 most awful experience.

Think about it for a moment—remember the first time the one-eyed snake entered the proximity of the prized jewel. Every boy was after it and some were very skilled at convincing the most dedicated virgin out of her panties. The frisky male spent countless hours talking on the phone, saying the right words to win the virgin's trust and then . . . BOOM–BAM, suddenly the two are setting up a date and time to implement the inevitable exchange.

I remember that day as if it were a rerun of my favorite episode. I cringe when I rehash every moment of the ten minutes it took to complete the whole deed. I often wish I had the power to blink myself back to that very moment so many years ago (stop looking for an exact age or year) so I can yell STOP and get myself the hell off of virginity massacre lane.

It started out as pure excitement, extreme arousal and tingling sensations from brushing against the breasts, sucking nipples, earlobes, rubbing testicles; thrashing tongues against the neck, lips, and ears; the sound of licking, smacking, moaning roaring then . . . BOOM–BAM, without warning, an uncontrollable erect mass of muscle was forcing through my innocence. Only one second of quiet to turn back, but then . . . BAM, it was too late. A small tear deflated my cherry and the uncomfortable pelvic thrusting, fast non-rhythmic movements, sloppy kisses, and bone-breaking repercussions were the only physical memories left from handing over a prize jewel.

Traumatized, overwhelmed, and confused, I thought I had finally been initiated into the world of sexual revolution. I actually thought if my COOCARACHA hurt when I walked on an angle for two days, I was blessed with a dude that could rock my world. HA! It was only a decade later, after the horrific experience that I would later find out having your COOCARACHA ripped away from the walls of your golden treasure didn't qualify as great sex.

* * *

The first kiss, first caress, the first magical session of foreplay was the most exhilarating experience I could ever imagine. It left me dizzy and light-headed as if I had ridden a booze cruise crossing into different continents on the border of the equator. One moment I was cool, the next moment I was burning up with a tingling sensation of sun-kissed butterflies flapping their weightless wings in circular motions from the nape of my neck down to my curly toes. The motion of fire, water, hot stones, and warm wind tunnels swirling up my spine, down to the treasure-filled chest, and then BAM, the lock popped without forced entry. A miniature violinist appeared floating in the air as we both squeezed each other tight to unite our rhythmic vibrations and just before the fat lady began to sing . . . a warm stream of summertime mist filled the space between the heart-shaped cheeks that outlined the soft indention of his and her sheets.

I'm so blessed to know the difference between child's play and the art of making soulful love with your soul mate.

Day 24:

My Ghetto Heaven

There's no place like my home, my 'hood, my block. It's the street where my footsteps can be sketched on a paper against the cracked sidewalk. The street that offers comfort, joy, and good ol' southern hospitality, and everybody knows your name. OK, OK . . . the place I'm talking about is about twenty miles southeast of Capitol Hill in the Nation's Capital.

My 'hood possesses traits that may arouse the media to portray as GHETTO. However, that's not what I remember. I grew up in *HEAVEN*—heaven on earth. I remember peaceful days of jumping double-Dutch rope with burgundy *Kangaroo* sneakers, playing hopscotch, and staining the sidewalk with love messages of grade school crushes . . . I (heart) *john, ron, and sean.*

I remember clutching my dollar that I begged my mother to give me as an advance on my allowance for chores that I hadn't really completed. I longed to hear the chiming bell of the ice cream truck that satisfied my daily crave for sour pickles, Pop Rocks, salt and vinegar potato chips, *Now & Later* candy, *Lemon Heads*, sunflower seeds, hot sausages, pickled pigs' feet (the pigs' feet were for my sister), and strawberry sodas. An hour later, I was scheming and plotting with my best friend to get an advance from her mom, because the soft serve ice cream truck just landed on the block.

My Heaven, my 'hood, is the place that brings memorable reflections of the days I spent playing hopscotch, tag, or freaky Friday. You know freaky Friday—the game where the skinny anorexic girls who haven't reached puberty run around the yard with their overly developed friends—hiding, whispering, and wishing that the neighborhood boys participating in the chase would grab them, and perform three dry humps in the midst of laughing and sweating. A smile creases my lips as I remember days and countless hours I spent shaking my imagination and struggling to successfully twirl the Hula-Hoop and keep it above my naturally straight bones.

My neighborhood was the cross between ghetto and the cream of the crop. It was a safe haven for me. The random yelling and laughing often heard from the torn screens outside thick squared paned windows would fill my heart with a weird comfort and solitude. My 'hood was the place where nice, rugged, scheming, hardcore, wholesome, and downright nasty folks were rolled up into one big Tootsie Roll. Everyone didn't get along all the time, especially teenage girls, and territorial boys. You would see heads rolling on top of skinny necks at 35mph, cutting —and the popping sound of air between teeth and cavities could be heard bouncing off the steam-filled streets, as the crackling voices of menstrual females gnarling at the bright sun would spit hateful insults at the other immature group of girls across the street. Tall, skinny, chubby, and short teenage boys caught a glimpse of a passerby who presented sketchy behavior, as the boys exuded boisterous displays of testosterone while seeking chance and opportunity, disrespecting their mothers' wishes by accepting risky opportunities to compete with their friends' expensive feet.

Pulse-racing memories often flood my heart when I stand in the midst of my old neighborhood and reminisce on the day I witnessed the first of many neighborhood battles between Jasper Place and First Street. I realized at a young age that even though everyone didn't get along within the quadrant sections of my 'hood, everyone (except me and other onlookers) stood together to unite and fight as one—but only when it was deemed necessary. It's the old family theory . . . you can't stand your family, sister or brother, but you'll beat anyone's ass that dares to disrespect one or all of them.

There's always a smell or sound that triggers my unforgettable memories, as I transport my son to visit Grandma. Perhaps it's a small peek of the sun fighting through the clouds, children's laughter, chatter of preadolescent girls draping their hips with a telephone cord they've converted into a jump rope to compete in a double-Dutch challenge—or little boys below the age of fourteen racing by on their *Mongoose* bikes, kicking up dirt and rocks that miss my windshield by one shift of the hot air.

Suddenly reality kicks in and promptly forces me to remember that time changes—just as a filthy old man in a brown van drives up slowly, winking his left eye at me, and staring at the crackhead fifty feet ahead with his right eye. I shake off the image of his intentions, and motion my son to walk fast to the gated building. I hastily remove us both from the potential broken memory of peace and good times. I guess I shouldn't discriminate, I'm sure there will be some crackheads, pimps, and drug dealers in heaven—or at least in my *Ghetto Heaven* on earth.

Day 25:

Crushed Beauty

The price to be beautiful is priceless . . . Hmmm, is it really? I believe all women are beautiful in their own way. Yes, we all have flaws like big feet, big butts, small breasts, big gigantic breasts, flat butts, wide hips, small feet, cute asymmetrical toes, big caveman toes, sausage toes, big noses, flat noses, huge foreheads, flat heads, dented heads, big teeth, missing teeth, rice-sized teeth, Chiclet-sized teeth; I mean the list can go on forever. Let's start with the price our feet pay to begin my witty analysis.

Imagine having the pressures of beauty weighing on your shoulders. You search the whole mall to find the perfect pair of shoes that would create a bold statement of beauty, only to find the perfect pair to be a half size too small. So what would you do? Well I should add that you're a seventeen-year-old high school student seeking the perfect shoe to wear to the prom. Hmmm! Have I sparked any jolts of long-term memory?

Well, think about this, have you ever watched a woman walk with both feet pointed inward (some would call it pigeon-toed)? Of course, some women are naturally cursed with the awkwardness of their toes greeting each other with every stride, but there are some that have altered their stride to accommodate their choice to wear the cutest pair of too-small shoes. Our feet can conform to any high-intensity situation; like being stuffed in a hot oven of thick leather uppers for hours—without room to stretch or reposition. I'm convinced that pigeon-toed women were the teenage girls stuffing their feet in the perfect, too-small dyeable shoes for the prom.

I remember being teased for having small breasts and big feet. Adolescents are horrible and each one takes the word of another as the written law of coolness. I wish I knew then what I know now as a confident, beautiful, small-breasted, big-foot adult woman. If there were a time machine in my garage, I would jump inside and revisit my past. I'd land on the shoulder of my twelve-year-old self and whisper words of guidance and assurance in my adolescent ear, as she (I) stood in the bathroom stuffing my training bra with tissue. I would tell her to ignore the pressures and just be herself (myself) and spare her (me) the mortifying moment hours later as she (I) sat in the doctor's office for a checkup. Just as her (my) doctor leaned in to check her (my) vital signs, he pulled the chain of tissue out of the bra for an accurate assessment.

Years later, I would whisper to the adolescent Savvy that buying the right size tennis shoes would spare (us) the two foot surgeries to remove the bunions that I swore were hereditary. Discomfort and misery are all I felt in my late twenties, when I couldn't care less what shoe size rocked my ankles and toes.

Go ahead, laugh out loud—but don't judge. I'm sure we've all altered our flaws to fit in and go along with the mold of nonsense. There are prob- ably females rushing off to work or school wearing jeans or slacks two sizes too small because they refuse to accept their beauty. The side seams are expanding, exceeding the shape and conform- ing to the forced alterations.

I'm so happy I'm now comfortable in my own skin, breasts, butt, and feet. At my tender age of thirty- something, I seek the pleasure of comfort, and now will even buy a half size bigger for my stilettos, peep toe pumps, and pointed-toe boots. I'm now sexy and comfy.

Day 26:

Cutting Eyes

It always amazes me to see the instantaneous hatred among women—young or old. Why can't we all just get along? Just smile when you pass me in the aisle of Wal-Mart, Target, or the grocery store; shit, I don't know you, your man, or your baby. I am living to survive just like you. It's not my fault your day is bad. I didn't wake up next to you and deprive you of a quickie under the sheets, or toothpaste to cover the stench, or eggs and bacon to fill your growling belly.

Fine wine perfects with age and my journey through life is perfecting me. I've begun analyzing the body language and behavior of all women, mostly African-American, but all in general. We all possess some duplicate traits that are negative and sketchy. Now, I am no saint, and will admit that earlier in my adolescent years and in between my young adult ages, I have sometimes behaved horribly while existing in the same space of unfamiliar human beings—mostly females. Whenever I was in the same atmospheric space of a female, whether she was a stranger, my arch enemy, or neutral peer, I would be overwhelmed with cattiness, lacking extreme class. Gossip sessions of whispers and chants were displayed with a side order of snickering and quick glances.

Now as a wise, fine-tuned, and buffed queen, I notice the same petty glances between hot-natured teen girls in their skinny jeans and tight T's. They walk around starving for attention from the roughneck boys that prompt the cutting eye wars. But don't shortchange your thoughts, the cattiness still exists in adult women as well. There are grown ass women who still harbor unnecessary traits that equate them with their teenage sisters, daughters, and nieces.

As women we consume the role of our own worst enemy. We deprive each other of compliments, pep talks, gratitude, apologies, motivation, inspiration, and pure love. It seems we would rather knock each other off the cliff we are all climbing together to reach a balanced life, efficiency, and solitude. When you step onto an elevator filled to capacity, it doesn't hurt to smile or nod hello.

We are all striving to succeed and the woman or girl you cut down with your razor sharp rays may be wearing the bootstraps that you need to grab onto in order to reach the top of your game.

I'm just saying . . . let's uplift one another!

Day 27:

Ambush Makeovers

Paranoia—I always think someone's following me. It's those days when I'm feeling raggedy, not focused, and not on guard, that I swear a FASHIONISTA and her camera crew are going to jump out of hiding and attack me.

I wish I could be glamorous 24/7, but it's impossible because I lack the luxury of employing a live in housekeeper, nanny, fitness trainer, and chauffer. That's a fairy tale that gets stomped on every morning as the sun and the moon kiss each other in passing. You would think the hairy werewolf howls as the beauty awakens. Ha! Not in this fairy tale of Savvy's Reality.

I roll out of bed and brush my face—wash my teeth with my eyes closed, and begin my morning ritual by bellowing for all to rise for breakfast, wardrobe changes, and carpool drop offs. It's so rhythmic I can do it blindfolded. Most often I feel I do, especially when I drive the hypnotic route to and from my son's school. Every morning while I sit in the carpool line waiting for the teachers to retrieve my child, a rush of panic rushes over me because I feel a stampede of FASHIONISTAS and their camera crews are surrounding my truck reaching for me. When my truck stops rocking from the stylish insurgents . . . I speed off with a full face of foundation, eye shadow, mascara, and lip gloss.

Of course I realize it was only a daydream when I pull into the parking lot of Wal-Mart. Damn. I close my eyes tight and wish the FASHIONISTAS would appear when I call because they're often summoned in my silent chants and prayers when I'm rushing through the doors of my favorite store, camouflaged in my sunglasses, sweats, and Crocs, focused on a covert mission to grab and dash the necessary items to maintain the household. I'm like a dope fiend ducking through aisles, trying to avoid the unforeseen circumstances of running into the *back in the day* high school friends. Why is it that every time you make the fatal choice to run to the store you see someone you've haven't seen in fifteen years?

I'm awakened from my fairytale trance of ducking and dodging from the voice of the cashier whose face is familiar. She takes a double glance and then begins spewing out "hello and how the hell are you?"

Damn, we both could use an unsuspecting Ambush Makeover!

Day 28:

It's Just One of Those Days . . . or Weeks!

Sleep, eat, pee, poop, sleep, eat, sleep, eat—pee, poop. That was the routine I easily adjusted to last winter during the biggest snowstorm of 2010. The daily routine of a life packed with high-energy, nonstop days of errands, household chores, school drop offs, and pickups; soccer, football, and basketball practices. An uninterrupted schedule of activity for others often prompts wishes of extreme timeouts.

The beginning of 2010 brought an unexpected burst of forceful blizzards and snowstorms that were welcomed with open arms by my household. The snowstorms gave the perfect opportunity for me to do nothing, and be nothing.

I was the laziest human being in the world. I added more meals, snacks, and beverages to my daily activity. The refrigerator and I became more acquainted each day. My love for cookies increased, and I didn't even care about the uninvited abrasions I would get from the hidden Oreo crumbs hiding in my sheets when rolling over. I didn't brush my hair, not even my teeth, and I didn't care. I am not ashamed to admit that my daily regimen of showers or baths decreased to every three days, often prompted by the quick whiff of stale aromas that forced me to make a mental revision to my *to-do-before-midnight* list. My animals were even privy to the down time. They slept more than me, and ate just as much. Our mornings began later, and our nights transitioned into mornings.

Haven't you had just one of those days when you wished the world would stop without cause and everyone would just chill the hell out? I'm convinced that when the earth shakes over twenty million snowflakes outside the doors of your home, you have the obligation to chill the fuck out. No questions asked. However, there should be a handbook for all to follow and pop quizzes should be given to children under the age of seven to test their knowledge of what school closures and government shutdowns actually mean. Yes, it is OK for our children to stay up late—because ultimately that means they will wake up later in the morning, which means you will wake up later. Waking up later will give you more time before they begin to demand full course meals for all three sessions of the day. The other benefit to late morning awakenings is that children begin to lose track of time, and soon their days seem like their nights. Eventually they will start eating all three meals at one time and you will have more time to chill the hell out.

So the next time *Mother Nature* decides to unleash a billion snowflakes on my lawn, in my neighborhood, and throughout my city—resulting in a time-out for everyone for two weeks—I am going to continue to rest my body, lay in my bed, eat all my Oreos, reacquaint myself with the refrigerator every half hour, drink all my stocked bottles of fine wine—poop, pee, sleep, poop, eat, sleep, poop, pee, eat, and sleep more, without cause, and let it be just one of those lazy days that count toward rebooting for the spring.

Day 29:

Fudge-Gin-Benches

Scrunch the words together, pronounce it fast and repeat it twice: Fudge Gin Benches, Fudge Gin Benches. Do you know of any? I guess the first step is for me to describe what they are and how a few Fudge-Gin-Benches have affected me.

Fudge-Gin-Benches had me spinning on their merry-go-round missions, tricking me into thinking I'm a wooden bench that's been scuffed up, walked on, spit on, lied upon, buffed down, smoothed out to shine . . . but only for the moment that's convenient for show.

Now I've always shared a bountiful batch of unconditional love for those who share the same prehistoric life of trials and tribulations—from pigtails, miniskirts, and asymmetric fashioned hair.

I've never judged those Fudge-Gin-Benches for all or any dysfunctional transgressions that are overlooked, hidden, and neatly tucked with a dangling string that always leads to the truth. It's no secret I'm different from you, you, you, you, and you. I'm not a crouch-less cougar, a laughing hyena, a psychotic nymphomaniac, a misinformed professional, a pathological liar, or even a self-absorbed inconsiderate hater. I'm the answer to those who seek understanding, openness, and thoughtfulness.

I've been excluded from the rocky whirlwind effects of your heartless actions, but you act as if your misery has besieged your world without notice. I stopped calling and unleashing my thoughtfulness . . . but I bet you, you, you, you, and neither you took a moment to notice. I'm tired of being second best, lied to, denied of, hated on, snickered about when you're liquored up on *Grey Goose* or wine, yet, your truths uncover hidden vulnerabilities. I've had it; no more predictable themes will be accepted from you, the art of overlooking and dismissing me for special occasions, birthdays, holidays, first dates, playdates, anniversaries, life-altering situations, marriages, divorces, bridal showers, baby showers—the list could continue for days.

You see, the cluster of Fudge-Gin-Benches will grow and fester in the construction of their internal design. I thought our history and unspoken loyalty would've prevented choices of adding your best friend's name to the third, fourth, or fifth draft of maiden choices. I swear you'll have to do a double take when déjà vu erupts the melodic flow of friendship and you've been kicked out of weddings, erased off contact lists, which lead to missed birthdays and the lack of calls to express condolences of personal deaths and misfortune.

* * *

I'm renewed, refreshed, and exuberant with the urge to dust the fallacies off my shoulder and remove myself from negative thoughts and intentional mis-understandings. We're cool, but I release you, you, you, you, and you from the sudden urges of unnec-essary spews. I was ignored through your silent treat-ments created by the clustered trilogy, yet the epic will probably continue without anyone noticing. But just as the plot thickens, an unspoken acknowledg-ment stands before us, which is probably why the unexecuted visits have multiplied into three-word texts, one sentence e-mails, and avoidance.

The tiredness exceeds my willingness to continue the boring trip on the merry-go-round clues and insults of whether I'm really a part of the faux don-key butt sisterhood. I've decided to break free from spinning and falling off of the seats of my favorite Fudge-Gin-Benches.

117

Day 30:

Cry Baby—Cry Mommy!

Why do we tell our children not to do certain things, especially when they've witnessed us acting out the same unacceptable behavior? We tell our children not to lie, cheat, steal, and most often not to cry—unless they're traumatically injured or sick on their deathbed. Yet, on a good day, they'll witness us wiping our tears away as we end an intense conversation with a neighbor. They'll catch the tail end of a meltdown while we're on the phone begging the utility company to extend the second deadline for back payments. We leave our children searching for answers when they walk in on us rolling on the hardwood floor crying out for help when threats of lawsuits, garnishments, and bankruptcy swirl around the brim of our halo, converting it into a sun visor cap.

Absorb this solution to our hypocritical revolution . . .
the next time your tantrum leaks out, walk your ass
over to a mirror while you're knee-deep in pain
and . . . snap out of it when you see your hypocritical snotty-nosed face. We want our children to
grow up to be strong, independent, unemotional
beings that walk a straight line of decency, yet we
allow them to absorb the many intentions of ducking calls from creditors and our ploys to ignore ringing door bells, avoiding certified letters for intent
to foreclose. Our sweet children soak up all of our
gossiping sessions on the phone as we chat about
the crazy ass family members who publicly put us
to shame, or the sidebar strategies to conjure up
the perfect schemes and angles for tax breaks we
think we can claim.

I'm amazed at the identical traits of my personality my "mini me" has inside of him. His intellec-
tual level and skillful ability to dissect, rebuild,
reason, and seek resolution for the many conversations he's soaked in over the years, add to his
intelligence of knowing exactly when to unleash
the most pertinent information and who to
reveal it to.

So the next time your child is rolling around screaming on the floor unleashing his closeted energy
of repressed emotions and rage; just ignore him.

But if you're having one of your weak and pitiful moments, lie down beside him and release the rage, erase the hypocrisy and unite the tantrums forever. Hold up the mirror, wipe off each other's snot and let your "mini me" know that it's OK to cry, baby . . . cry, Mommy!

Day 31:

My American Idol

For the past sixty-seven seasons, she's topped the popularity charts as a platinum beauty, graced with charisma, featured with passionate eyes. She seduces her fans with a magnetic field of unconditional love, understanding, trust, and resilience. I've been a true fan of this idol for more than thirty years. She's my hero, my ace . . . she's the whole package of prosperity, solidarity, confidence, wisdom, and grace. Her presence fills any room with joy and warmth.

My American Idol's wisdom ignites a fuel in me to be the best. I'm intrigued with her ability to exude calmness and patience under the most extreme stress. I'm her biggest fan. I'm the first in line for every sold-out show to receive her dose of wisdom, advice, and wit; headlined with resolution for drama, punishment, discipline, cat fights, broken hearts, petty arguments, disorderly conduct, and insult. Without her knowledge and experience, I would've been a hopeless, naïve, shallow, dependent, lost, and confused individual.

Her message of independence, security, purpose, patience and common sense has given me the edge that keeps me armed with grace and sustainability.

I'm so glad that I won the lifetime VIP backstage pass to receive an endless amount of her love and nurturing touch, laced with priceless hugs, and soft cheek kisses. She's my mother, my favorite DIVA, my Best Friend, my American Idol.

Day 32:

Arguments

Frustrations and unforeseen circumstances are often the key ingredients to arguments. Well that's my theory, and I'm sticking to it. I'm the laid back, easygoing half of the relationship—but my man would argue that he carries the laid back title of our relationship. I can honestly say, my man and I never argue. We sing tunes of frustration, and then we kiss. Except for that one particular cloudy day where the sun peeked through the clouds as if it were playing hide and seek with mother earth. I was already displaying signs of my other personality due to the arrival of my annoying *Aunt Dot*. She arrives just when I am feeling so sexy, lovable, and irresistible. He knows how I am, especially when my annoying relative (Aunt Dot) pops up, uninvited.

So the day went something like this—I was bathing our child. After his bath, I began the ritual of caring for his dry skin by massaging and soothing then lubricating with hypnotic motions of scented ointments. My beautiful baby was finally calm and relaxed, just seconds away from slipping into a deep sleep, when suddenly *Daddy* pops his head in full view, distracting baby boy. My nostrils begin to flare, but I bite my lip to prevent the slip of my tongue; besides, baby boy is spewing out a foreign language that oddly sounds exactly like the words that I really wanted to speak.

This intelligent man just ignored all the signs; instead, he continues to push all my wrong buttons by saying things like, "Did you cook?," "Did you wash my blue shirt?" and "Are you gonna take care of big Daddy tonight, Mommy?" Twenty seconds later, he is wiping water off of his face, slipping on the hardwood floors, and blinking his eyes uncontrollably because of the dripping water weighing down his eyelashes.

Now he realizes something is wrong. He walks away, leaving me inside the house, with our babbling baby, which increases my frustration. I open the window, and lean into the screen, yelling out words I have never heard or written. He laughs, jumps in his car, and drives off.

I snap out of my altered personality and can't comprehend what happened. Thirty minutes later, my sweetie arrives with cartons of shrimp with snow peas, brown rice and chicken with broccoli. I run into his arms, hug him and whisper soothing tunes of love in his ears. He looks at me with confusion, and then we kiss. The night was perfect, with my sweetie and our babbling baby. I look into his eyes and say to him, "I'm glad we never argue—instead, we just kiss our frustrations away."

Day 33:

Hoarders—Just Let it Go!

I'm surrounded by many items in my home, that have started to pile up around certain hub spots like the basement, the kitchen and the family room (small controllable piles), but all of the items have become unnecessary frustrations that haunt me in my sleep. Perhaps if I'd learned to recycle more at an earlier age, I wouldn't harbor these thoughts. The three main items that force me to grind my teeth on a daily basis are . . .

Underwear—my underwear is categorized under two headings . . . *menstrual cycle gear* and *just comfortable*. So why is my dresser drawer stuffed with underwear that I know won't fit around one thigh, yet alone my right or left butt cheek? But I still hold onto them. Perhaps I'm awaiting that sudden rush of feeling *Grown and Sexy*.

Clothes—I am ashamed to even admit to having clothes tucked away in the closet with the price tags still intact. I just keep transferring the garments from the storage bins to the closets each season—hoping next season my hips, torso, or thighs will allow me to wear them once and be uncomfortably snug.

Receipts—three black trash bags full of receipts that display dates from eight years ago. For some reason, I've convinced myself that I may need one of the receipts to return an item that I may or may not have used. Seriously, I want to shake myself silly when I find a roll of three-year old receipts after deciding to transfer all my nonsense of necessities out of one purse to another. I just shake my head and continue to transfer the roll to the next purse in line.

I'm sure if I pondered more deeply, my list would increase by the hour, leaving me to shake my head shamefully at the ridiculous list of items. Here are a few more to think about . . .

Cell phones—how many times have you upgraded to keep up with the latest release? Well I can count on both hands the number of random cell phones from different phone providers that have become my son's toy phones. I look back and wonder why did I need so many upgrades of a flip phone, slide phone, and of course . . . the smart phone. If it was so smart, why didn't I keep it? Hmmm!

Old keys—I have resided in more than three locations, and yet the keys to my first, second, and third apartment are still attached to the keys that unlock the door to my new home. Really, I just have to release and don't look back. It cracks me up; if I threw the old keys away, perhaps my purse wouldn't be so heavy. Do people really throw away keys though? Hmmm!

Music CD covers—Just throw them away. The amount of space they hold could be used to store more unnecessary items.

The list can go on and on, so JUST LET IT GO!

Day 34:

Socially Frustrated

I'm often sent on an emotional roller coaster of bullshit and drama; a basis that lacks purpose and is filled with impersonal electronic disconnections. LOL, OMG, IDK, BRB, ROTFLMAO.

These random acronyms are lazy written emotions of short gestures of communication between individuals who'd rather socialize via text or on social network platforms. Individuals who base their status and popularity on the number of friends they have stamped on their profile. The politics of numbers and virtual engagements are a joke to me. I'm someone who values quality time and true friendship, who'd rather puke up notebook pages or a one-page typed letter than to feed all the hungry egos.

I love the intimacy between the stroke of my pen and crisp journal paper as the ink appears with each rhythmic vibration of mixed script and cursive. I love the external release of my inner thoughts and emotions about a particular person, event, or celebration. A note written to someone special just to say hello or thank you is obsolete. I am the first to condone and glorify the convenience of instant technology—but only to a specific 90 degree angle. My mind is quick and crafty so I will take advantage of our elaborate technology to send a detailed e-mail to those whom I've considered to be worthy of my friendship. They're the ones I will set extra time aside to call on the phone and verbally exclaim HAPPY BIRTHDAY, MERRY CHRISTMAS, CONGRATULATIONS, and even saddened CONDOLENCES. The intimacy and personalization is eradicated when special moments are acknowledged with a text. It's amazing how many friends I used to call true friends are now categorized into the cold disconnected friend list box on my Facebook profile. Now they're sharing space with associates I've met in passing; whether at work or in other social settings. My Facebook page is really used to connect virtually with an unattached but socially integrated world of nosy people.

I don't want to receive a HAPPY BIRTHDAY only on my wall from the group of people I've called my friends. Pick up the damn phone and interact with me. What happened to the personable interaction that created our realistic friendships? You'd rather minimize your interaction to less than 140 characters and tweet me your updated status. I'm not surprised though—the element of communication was never a strong foundation that molded our connection. Our history is full of partying, drinking, dancing, and capturing those moments in photos.

Guess what, followers . . . I'm unplugging the hype dream connections, disconnecting from the digital realm of social addiction. I'll de-friend my real friends and update my status to UNPLUGGED. So the next time your inner being wanders awake from the digital pack and you begin to crave human interaction, send me an old-school friend request. Reconnect with your pen or grab a connection from your landline receiver to engage and react through the revolutionary vibrations of laughter and auditory reception—shared between real friends. OMG, U R SO FUNNY, ROTFLMAO!

I guess a virtual world of digital interaction and social addiction is the best platform to fuel your socially connected false reality. I'm unplugging my profile, I Won't Be Back! PEACE!

Day 35:

It Takes a Village . . .

The beating drums, African horns, babies, mamas, grandmas, and great-grandmas surround the circle of life in the woods. A village is a community comprised of a cluster of women and men that fill the cavity to develop and strengthen the young. This is my understanding of family and the extension of . . .

My neighborhood is full of support, and as a child I never appreciated the internal beauty within the folds of cohabitation—whether single, double, or overcapacity. It was filled with women who'd experienced their share of strobe lights, catty-fights, disco mania, and baby mama/baby daddy drama. No matter what, all the women stuck together like a herd of penguins protecting the young from lurking predators.

During the summer days you would find me and other cool kids playing hopscotch, double-Dutch rope, or skating up and down the sidewalk on balled wheels made for indoor skating. All day we would rip up and down the street laughing and cracking on Bubblicious gum, soaking up the sun and whizzing past the drunken wine heads who were vigilant about patrolling the 'hood and protecting all who were part of the fine fabrics woven together as one. They knew every child's name and to whom we all belonged.

The pimps and their moneymakers were good people too . . . they would spend their days napping on the side of the buildings, but when dusk approached, the half-dressed fast tails winked once and suddenly *"Lights, Camera, Action."* The shiny cars would line up for at least twelve hours of curbside entertainment.

If there weren't any summer day camps in session, our parents could rely on the neighborhood mother who spent her days collecting checks on the first of the month from the government. She was ol' reliable. Let's call her Ms. Pat. Ms. Pat would sit in the living room window all day smoking on her Salem cigarettes puffing the smoke through the screen, and watching her soap operas in between. She made sure we ate our breakfast on the porch and called us in for a quick peanut butter and jelly sandwich for lunch. When Ms. Pat's shift ended upon the strike of 5:00 p.m., she would yell for her daughter to take her daily field trip to the liquor store to buy more Salems. Our field trip often brought on brief reunions with crackhead cousins, Alcoholic Anonymous rejects, and our favorite neighborhood street braider who'd confirm our weekend porch side appointment in passing.

There was a role for everyone, and they all played their own deck of cards well. The alcoholic duo, Uncle Sid and Uncle Ben, would teach us the "art of knowing how to hold your liquor" and tips on never mixing whites and browns together. They would yell in unison, "Take it straight to the back of your throat with no chaser and gasp for air."

The street hustlers taught us the value of entrepreneurship and how to resist a corporate gig. Mr. Pimp-'licious always thought he was giving us lessons we'd never consider: "Stay in school, keep your head up, and stay off the damn pole." Of course we were wise enough not to trust his ass, or Candy the crackhead and Vicki the fiend. They would catch you walking out of the store and beg for $5, $10, or $40. Now how are you gonna ask twelve- and thirteen-year-old kids for $40? But knowing them had a few perks, like the days or weeks when our mothers were recycling the

139

leftover meals—they would knock on our doors in the nick of time to sell big ass T-bone steaks and live whole chickens. I'm still wondering where the hell they got live chickens.

Now, I can't forget Rose and Tiny, the magnificent, rude ass, self-indulgent *air-benders*. They were a part of the village and fulfilled no real purpose but somehow managed to fit in without notice. They walked slowly, swinging their hands backward, bending the air, and crushing the mood of everyone they surrounded. Sidewalks cracked and stairs trembled, alerting innocent bystanders of their arrival accompanied by rudeness and hunger. Rose and Tiny were kind at times but their focus was destruction . . . destruction of delectable steaks and chickens.

* * *

At night when the sunset dimmed the block and the streetlamps blazed bright, my crew and I would run like refugees climbing over stone-covered mountains seeking shelter. We would plow through the front door of one of our houses— depending on which of our mothers was scheduled to kill, clean, bake, and fry the chicken and steak. Once all the children were fed and nestled all in one bed, the late night card game/dance party would begin. A few secretive knocks at the door and peep hole confirmations would prompt the catwalk to shine the spotlight on a few pimps and their bitches, wine heads, crack fiends, pot-heads, air-benders, welfare mamas, ex-con daddies, hustlers, drug dealers, and government working citizens. They all gathered in the kitchen, cracked opened a few decks of cards, smoked their cigarettes, lit their incense, danced to the jumping needle on the record, and drank their Colt 45 and straight Hennessy or cheap gin.

The whole village fellowshipped together under one roof without false pretenses or high expectations—just a village taking care of one another.

Day 36:

Trigger Words

So many words are spoken . . . some slow, some fast, and some dangle at the edge of your inner ear allowing enough time to digest the tone and delivery. The other words and full sentences are ignored as a massive traffic jam of conversation halts leaving dead air and echoes of crickets. Your friends, co-workers, arch enemies, or whoever you're talking to at that moment, begin to notice your disfigured facial expressions covered with oozing steam from your ears. That one repulsive word has stopped everything.

Words like SWEETIE exiting the lips of the co-worker who you only speak to in passing or when you're forced to work with on an extensive project erects every strand of hair on your body. The word SWEETIE is used only by my Auntie Bea or Marie, not by someone who knows nothing about me, never asked personal questions, or shared personal issues with me.

What about the co-worker that shortens your name as if she or he walks in the same shoes as your favorite office crew? The crew, who have permission to call me Jah, exclaim it with pleasant smiles. Listen up co-worker, you aren't my buddy, so stop trying to fit in—you're just setting me off.

It takes a lot of small annoyances to set my hot temper to volcanic erosion. The eruptions of my explosive temper is usually set off by the verbal taunts spoken with dramatic intentions like, BITCH, SLUT, MUTHA FUCKA, or a bold FUCK YOU. I am no saint, and admit these words have slipped through the tight corners of my lips, shedding off layers of my innocence—but I strive to replicate a soul destined to stand beside a saint. However, my game points are always deducted when a chick or a dude challenges me to a verbal shoot-out.

It normally begins with a magnetic field drawing me in to negate my drama free day. Joy is in the air and internal pitches of melodic beats are fueling the peppy stride my feet formulate. A glimpse a few yards ahead locks in on a group of socially dysfunctional male humanoids that fills the space I'm destined to pass. A few corny greetings fill the atmosphere and bellows of charismatic responses are exchanged. But of course there is always the one black sheep of the crew . . . the one sheltered being that was absent when bags of respect, dignity, and socially correct cues were dispersed in school—or home. The black sheep bellows out the one word, which, without a doubt, sends my neck into a whiplash mode, spinning like the demonic exodus chick. The fearless thug in me unleashes the vocabulary battle.

* * *

Then . . . after all the smoke clears and the random ball of hay rolls past my feet, the social rejects are left in dismay, scratching their heads in amazement. I always surprise myself, acknowledging the beast in me as my adrenaline pumps fast through my veins. I wonder which words of my fiery spews triggered the social misfit's cues. Do the words HELLO, FINE, THANK YOU, NO THANK YOU, and HELL NO ignite signals of dysfunction in the brain of those who can't function where free speech is spoken?

I believe if everyone recognizes the vocabulary triggers that send our emotions on a whirlwind ride, and we communicate the vocabulary dos and don'ts preferred by others; respect will eventually resonate in all of us—and we'll all become socially correct.

Day 37:

Desperately Seeking Savvy . . .

Upon the predictable rise of the sun, I awaken with an unbalanced rhythmic vibration in the center of my core. My eyelids flutter in distress from all of the wasted fluid leaking uncontrollably from the night before. Invisible holes outlining exit strategies of my energy can be traced from each attempt to raise my head away from the pillow. The ringing phone alerts my inner psyche that there are no more seconds left to ponder. I grab the sheets and throw them upward sending a giant wind tunnel of gray cotton enveloping the sleeping fur balls at my feet. Stepping out of bed is a tough job—but someone's gotta do it. I speak softly to myself, rebooting the ounce of confidence that resides in my mind, "You can do it—just do it." Stepping into the bathroom, turning lights on, and zooming into focus on the image in the mirror forces me to do a double take.

Who is this woman I see? She's a stranger, unfamiliar to me, though her features seem warm and friendly. A round-faced, caramel-complexioned woman with almond eyes, heart-shaped lips, and a button nose, but she doesn't look familiar. She's aged, annoyed, anxious, beat down, burnt out, challenged, confused, destroyed by flying pebbles of life, despised, degraded, disappointed, insecure, irritated, repulsed, run down, and tested. But I'm not convinced this is the woman I was raised to be, so I take a step back and glance at myself from a wider angle and lean in close for the kill. As I lean in closer, I notice a sparkle in my right pupil. It glistens with hope and joyful images of happy times, golden moments and elation. Snapshot reflections of myself appear; it's me, the Savvy Diva in her glory. I am her, she is me, I/we, are the perfection of the master above, the *High Almighty Heavenly Father.*

"I AM, I AM!" These words flow from the edges of my lips and I begin chanting like a spiritual monk given permission to speak. I AM . . . I AM . . . I AM . . . Jahzara, the most high of her QUEENDOM. I am the beginning to progression and success. I'm the end to all oppression that denounces my TRUE BEING. I reclaim my throne. I AM . . . I AM . . . I AM Just Me!

Day 38:

Identity Theft . . .

Have you ever awakened from a restless sleep and felt lost and incomplete? You feel weak, lonely, sad, and most often you long for a good night's sleep. You're nodding right now, not even realizing you're gone awake. You know something is missing but you can't put your finger, your life, your name, your thoughts, or even your money on it.

I feel like something is missing all the time, and it leaves me on a blindfolded search for validation or even a plug to fill a void. Then one day I realized I was seeking Spirituality. Seeking validation to express my true being, my woes, my pains. I began to explain . . .

* * *

SEX, my stress, the color of my skin . . .
Mental PARALYSIS conceals my world.
I can't escape, I can't run but I SCREAM!
I'm so scared, I SCREAM!
Numbness, anxiety is in control,
I can't breathe but see my heart pulsate.

Many STORMS I've weathered, but this I can't
win—for raindrops drench my tears.
Steel walls bridge gaps of communication even
bullets can't pierce.
I can't think, I can't think, when will it end.

Understanding I seek, relief I desire.
Boss Man lacks sympathy, my engine just blew, I
missed several work days and my family screams,
"I need you!"

Brothers and sisters chase the white devil, seeking
false fixes.
Surrender, Surrender I beg without selling your soul.

My jobless love seeks purpose—squeezing his manhood tight, so I keep him to fulfill my WOMANHOOD.

I can't bare it, my unstoppable tears,
Everyone's burdens I can't hold,
Weakened shoulders, I just can't hold.
Parallel Universes, I've heard of some,

It must be true—
Opposite mirrors images I see in blue.

Oh! SWEET SERENITY . . .
I awake on a sand-less beach with floating rocks,
swimming birds, graceful chirps—
gentle currents stain basins.
I'm WEIGHTLESS and HAPPY!

Tranquil harps distant in my ear,
Pink, Yellow, Blue, all I see;
Birds floating gracefully around me,
An angelic seagull rests upon me,
BREATHE, she said, BREATHE.

I awoke WEIGHTLESS and ENERGIZED,
Mother screaming, "Where have you been?"
Mr. Boss demanding reports—
Brother and Sister . . .
Well, they're still searching for the devil.

Reminiscence of Angelic Visions,
Repetitions of tickling tunes, exclaiming—
Don't give in. Everything will be all right!

Day 39:

Best in Show

A 10, 10, 10, and another 10 . . . A perfect score to define the qualifications of what most contests or competitions qualify as the best.

Hmmm! It's been my experience that you have to look deep within the characteristics, traits, or personality of any being to judge his or her will to succeed—right? It's a doggy, dog world, and all dogs give their best, especially when they know the spotlight is on them and the golden prize has been revealed.

I'm sure you've watched the BITCH as she stands with grace, perfection, and discipline. She holds her head high, arches her back and flexes her tightly defined thoroughbred legs and thighs, as the light sparkles reflections of healthy shimmery hair. Her display of great posture and stamina leaves everyone in awe as she sashays her hips, frolicking in front of the world. Her presence makes other bitches bow out gracefully, and every stud remains standing tall, strong, and firm on stage.

Oh, she's good! She's practiced the art of running in circles with her tail in the air, luring in everyone to eventually fold.

I'm sure by now you've remembered seeing this bright-eyed bushy-tailed, erect-standing, quarterly nymphomaniac who dispels her unmeasured potion on unsuspecting studs, wagging her backside upward and downward, backward, forward, and down again. OK, OK—she's the BITCH who always steals the crown. The one whose bark or growl is sharply precise as her bite. I know you've seen her trotting through your place of work, leading a pack of sniffing studs stumbling behind her goods. She's so prissy at times it truly defines how calculating her thoughts of winning are every time. She's the one that seems to shine exactly when a herd of other bitches deserve the prize.

OK, if I haven't triggered any memorable moments, I'll clue you in this one last time. The BEST IN SHOW QUEEN is the undeserving BITCH that blinds onlookers, forcing them to ignore everyone else who is really working hard behind the scenes trying to accomplish their dreams. She's rotten to the core, and will ride any un-tucked shirttails to raise her from the basement of the career ladder, and knows exactly when to play the role of "Ms. I didn't mean to" victim. She'll play the role when she's backed into the offices of the fed-up, burnt-out, overworked, underpaid, *Top Dog* who really runs the show but was pushed off the ladder.

The politics of the office rules, guidelines, and personal benefits will always BENEFIT the one who shines bright as she steals the title and wears the crown, while everyone who should've been counted shamefully bows down as the underdog to the BITCH—lagging behind to forever sniff her ass.

Day 40:

In My Shoes . . .

In her shoes, not mine. My adolescence deeply yearned to wear a sole of another. I failed to know my style. I lived those "squeeze to fit" days, wearing tight upper leathers—not stitched for me.

See, I often pondered about them, she and he. What flavor does his love brew for her? What seasoning does he hide from me?

Bulging bunions and aching toes began to birth a fashion of maturity.

I'd whisper silently to myself, "Embrace Yourself, let go and set your toes free. Besides, you ain't she."

She's common, no funk or spunk—just chunk. Her style definitely stumbled from choices of chunky heels to leaning loafers.

Clarity revealed—Uniqueness is in! I'm the predator of style . . . the perfect shoe is my prey. DESIGNER SHOE WAREHOUSES leave my mouth salivating for air.

A love I devour . . .

But all soles don't appease my crave.

Only pointed, open, peep toe heels . . .

It's just what my sense of fashion reveals.

It's no secret, my feet—not PETITE.

My toes stretched from birthing my PRINCE. My ankles used to sport a cute size eight, now I'm pushing a nine, OK . . . maybe a ten.

But, you see, history is my moment in time.

Cravings of pointy leather and sassy stitched frames, giving this Goddess leverage, but not for fame.

I'm an eagle perched with ease, defeating the daily grind of my life as a QUEEN.

I am a co-provider, the lover, the aunt, the sister, the daughter, the MOTHER, the SEED who . . .

Helps pay the bills, feeds the young, supports all dreams of hard work undone—just as the moon peeks out.

My shoes can't be filled, only customized for my feet. I'm that hated CHICK rocking two-, three-, maybe four-inch heels.

Attention all hating heathens—You can't strut my walk. My shoes were sewn for ME, not you. Whether POINTED, OPEN, or PEEP, My toes strut with ease. I'll never again try on your shoes, living uncomfortably, unable to breathe . . .

I'll forever walk in these soles . . . in style just for ME!

DAY 41:

Forever 21

Forever twenty-one, forever young, I wish time could be frozen for special moments. Hmmm! I really call it Forever 2010 . . . 2010 because that's the only way I fit in, 'cause the ten puts me back on the platform of reality, or on a preserved shelf for the finest wines.

Ten years ago I was further away from ten years past now. It was such an easy going life of wearing fitted size six jeans, now it will take a miracle to squeeze uncomfortably in a size 10 . . . you see, 10 is the magic number for good and bad history. Historical times I recall as I could party nonstop to the break of dawn, all weekend, and every night of the week. My girls and I would slow down long enough to eat, shit, and shower—then sleep maybe two hours before rushing off to work.

Now my days of club hopping consist of hopping back and forth to the boys and girls club for football, soccer, and basketball practices and games. A night out with the girls isn't as easy as before, because we spend more time planning conference calls only to determine what time we'll call each other back to choose a designated driver.

I remember I would never miss an opportunity to spontaneously unleash some naked energy. Now I have to dream, plan, and schedule accordingly to get in a nighttime or morning quickie.

Calorie counting wasn't a forefront vocabulary word on my plate of healthy, hearty eating. It was just a matter of eating whatever was cheap enough to continue living. Nowadays, I'm dissecting carbohydrates, deducting fat grams, and making life-altering decisions in drive-through lines, or on the phone ordering pizza. Geez, I feel so ancient, always reminiscing on life as I once lived. Ten years ago, and ten years before. I'll just continue to long for more and more of those younger days when I could put away a six-pack of cupcakes and not see a bulging belly.

Acceptance is key, but not my reality. I have to make the choice to hold onto my past or keep screaming for a future to be FOREVER twenty-one.

Friendships of a Lifetime

How many friends have entered into, departed from, or remain in your circle of friends? If you are like me (someone that embraces everyone I meet, and click with instantly) then you probably have or perhaps had a lot of friends—that you've welcomed into your hallway of friendship. The only way these friends fit into our lives really depends on the type of "*Season*" you have faced, or are facing now. Some friends were perfect for the moment, and some will always be a permanent facet in your life. The three friends described in these last three sections will ignite some resemblance in the friends that most women can attest to knowing.

* * *

Day 42:

Where are All My Haters?

HATER-ADE! Have you tasted that sickening drink that makes you hate everything? I'm sure you've guzzled down a gallon of *HATER-ADE* once or twice; it sparks bitterness inside you, as you wish failure and disaster upon everyone—well at least that one person who ruffles your feathers.

I would like to introduce you to the Jealous/ Envious friend. The one we've grown to love, or perhaps the one we've become. We all have friends that get excited when they see the walls crumble around us—or they're happiest when they see us scrambling on the ground, scurrying to find ourselves. They feel weak and bitter when we're on top of our game, excelling beyond expectation—even our own. They secretly enjoy wallowing in our failures and go into an anorexic meltdown if we are doing anything that doesn't make them look good.

Now some of us won't admit it, but there have been times we experienced a little dose of envy and a double dose of jealousy. Take a moment to recall.

It may have been the day you realized your hair didn't wave up like your best friend's hair when you both were both caught in a thunderstorm (after your mother spent an hour pressing your hair in the hot, sticky kitchen); or perhaps it was the day you and your friend were trying on clothes in Bloomingdale's, and you glanced at her perfect body curving to the true shape of the jeans like a glove. Disappointment resonated over your face as your refection appeared in the mirror, displaying your underdeveloped body drowning in every pair of jeans you choose.

You may have secretly put a wad of bubblegum on her pillow as she slept during your weekly slee-povers, praying she'd roll over, locking the wad between her wavy locks; or perhaps you forgot to mention to her that her fabulous glove-fitting jeans were saturated with a questionable red stain covering the middle of her back pocket. I am not too proud to admit that I have suffered from a viral plague of jealously in my past—but who hasn't?

Even now as an adult, I still communicate with a few "jealous" plagued women. We all know one—let's call our jealous friend Melanie—I'm sure you've met. She is the friend you have known since before you two could speak or walk. You've shared your hopes, dreams, fears, desires, and yes, you've even made the fatal mistake of showing her a pair of shoes at the mall you've been eyeing—only for her to blatantly purchase the same pair on the spot. You love her like a sister—well, now your love for her is like the family member that you wish didn't come around so often, so you didn't have to hide your true self, in fear of your identity being stolen because of jealous tendencies.

Melanie is the one that you look for in a crowd as you are being awarded for an honorable achievement, but her jealousy got the best of her, so she skips the ceremony—but to be fair, she manages to make a cameo appearance at the reception three hours later; just as everyone is beginning to clean up. She is so overwhelmed with jealousy that she doesn't even realize that through all of your adolescent awkwardness and teenage trials, you always admired her for being witty, confident, and sincere. She's a fast talker, often loud and magnetic all in one breath—which she displays only when the spotlight is on her. She has a negative opinion about everything that puts a sparkle in your eye, and will take on your ideas as her own. She's also the friend who was cursed with voluptuous breasts in the seventh grade, wearing a "CC" cup bra. You often found yourself standing in the mirror, chanting, "I must, I must, I must increase my bust . . . I know, I know they soon will grow." Of course, Melanie told you that this chant would surely help the little knots on your chest expand in size like her *double c melons*. She would snicker in amusement as she lay across your bed watching your repetitive chant, and hold back the laughter as she tried to convince you that your knots were larger that day than the previous week.

You gotta love Melanie. She is the friend we will forever look forward to seeing on days when we feel down, because her jealousy will boost our ego. She harbors jealousy for no apparent reason, which will probably increase the day she meets another woman tainted with jealous tendencies—and the cycle will go on, and on.

* * *

So my rambling thought process has prompted my real question—how many of us still suffer from jealousy? Most of us have been psychologically shaped by past experiences, and we magically begin to embrace our flaws and assets. See, I am happy to acknowledge that my booty is my BIGGEST asset, and my mini cleavage is a small flaw for me. This flaw often causes me to experience slight setbacks, especially when one of my close friends is flaunting her "ta tas" on one of my bad days "to-be-a-small-chest-woman-because the-bikini-top-is-too-baggy."

But I'm not jealous at all. Recognizing my flawed body just prompts me to avoid facing forward in a crowded room when my friend's overflowing cleavage is overshadowing my presence. I always angle myself either sideways or with my back facing the crowd to let my asset outshine their frontal overload.

Day 43:

Blame It on the Tequila, Wine, and Beer!

I'm sure you've heard this phrase at least once or twice from someone in your circle, "What happened last night?" Or perhaps you're the one who's asked that question. Admit it—seriously, no judgment.

Everyone has a friend like Trina. She's the friend who never remembers what happened the night before. She weighs about 135 lbs. and swears she can hold her liquor or drink anyone under the table—including 300 lb. men. She's the bubbly chick that everyone loves to have around, especially in a social setting that includes a bar, music, a dance floor, and of course, Buffalo wings. The one you have to constantly keep an eye on in the

club, or at happy hour, or even at your office holi-
day party. Oftentimes, you wonder why the hell
you are out with her, because you never have the
chance to enjoy yourself.

Your "girls night out" planning normally starts out
with a conference call of excited divas deciding
on a few important factors for the night; like who
will drive, who's house will be the meeting spot,
and of course what outfits will accommodate the
mood of the night. After hours of planning and
finalizing all the key elements, everyone wonders
how the hell Trina's house was the final option for
the meeting spot, and why she is already mois-
tened with sweat beads dripping down the side-
lines of her face from three abnormal shots of
tequila. She's walking around the house nonchalantly; half dressed with a thong, stilettos and no
top—exclaiming that she can't find her favorite
party shirt. So of course we instantly realize that
the original plan of Trina chauffeuring the party
divas to the club instantly goes to *plan B*—which is
normally (someone like me) the person who feels
obligated to ensure the safety of everyone since
the rest of the divas have begun to throw back
shots of tequila to fight off the urge to attack Trina.

Everyone except the newly designated driver is
laughing, spewing unfamiliar language of excitement and demanding the driver to accelerate

the speed to rush the delivery of the four drunken divas to the club. Trina is the first one on the dance floor, the first to lose a shoe, a piece of clothing, and the first to be snatched off another woman's man after being spotted with her tongue down his mouth; and of course, the only one the other divas have to peel off the dance floor when the club lights begin flickering the closing signal.

The process of hydrating her with fluids begins before departing the bar and continues at her house into the early hours of the next morning. The morning greets the dedicated crew with a refreshed—but half-dressed Trina, who questions why everyone looks so worn out. She never believes the outrageous nights of her untamed excitement and expelling rants of vomit in cars that don't belong to her. The other divas spend all their morning trying to piece together some parts of the night for her, but most of the night is a blur to them as well.

Perhaps you're the one, just as I am, who grins in delight at the end of these adventures, because my best friend, the *Flip* camcorder, always helps me capture and preserve those precious moments.

I guess being the designated driver definitely has its perks!

Day 44:

Recycled Girls

Recycled lately? Though I've made a pact with my seven-year-old to help save the earth by separating plastics and aluminum trash for our yellow recycle bin—I've decided to recycle other things in life as well. I pondered this thought almost every day for the past six months, as I evaluated friendships that I once had with other women, and had recently vowed to never care about—Ever! It's amazing how the smallest or largest impacts on life can make you eat your words. I fashion myself as being hardcore when I vow to never speak to someone again—I am the queen of *Grudges*. I guess fortunately for me, I have been forced to realize all the creative energy I used to prove to these ex-friends was being wasted on nonsense. I would talk about the infamous fall that brought our friendship to its knees over, and over again to other friends—never realizing that I was the only person that was convinced these friendships didn't mean the world to me.

Eating my words was a tough act to endure, especially when I wasn't sure why the friendships ended.

Standing in front of Goldie's casket—one of my favorite friends, my cousin, my Best Friend Forever (BFF)—clarified one thing for me about holding grudges: it's just not that serious! I stood there starring at her lifeless body, wondering how I would go on through life without her pep talks, her laughter, her witty sense of humor, her straightforwardness, and her loving heart. I kissed her forehead several times before getting enough strength to walk away to leave her in the funeral home all alone. It was the hardest moment in my life. As I mustered up enough energy in my muscles to walk away, I looked back at her casket, and then pictured myself there in her place. The only question that hovered over me for the rest of the day was what impact would I have on those who loved me and those who once loved me as a friend?

I vowed to put aside my pride and reach out to the two women whose friendships once meant the world to me.

The whole experience of losing one of my best friends brought me bitter but sweet results. I mourn Goldie each and every day, and some days are harder than most—especially when I run across a photo of her, or Christmas card, or even hear her voice whisper behind me. The sweet ending in my loss allowed me to gain a new outlook on life. I have put aside all of my petty issues, insults, name-calling, and even jealous tendencies that perhaps were half the reason the two friendships were tossed away, with the intentions of leaving them in the trash bin.

Fortunately for me, my seven-year-old son's innocent outlook on life and the reason for recycling impacted my decision to pull the friendships up from the rubble and recycle them as well. Mashing and ironing out the past, renewing the friendship, and starting fresh from the recycled scraps of reasoning and forgiveness, has allowed me to appreciate the women they are now, as opposed to who we all were in our early twenties. Our friendships have traveled full circle from good to bad—transforming into something better.

Recycling was once a daunting task in my everyday life—but in the end, we can all benefit from reusing and re-purposing the treasures we already have in our lives!